W9-AVJ-641

The Hostage

Nancy Rue

BETHANY HOUSE PUBLISHERS
MINNEAPOLIS, MINNESOTA 55438

A Focus on the Family book
Published by Bethany House Publishers
A Ministry of Bethany Fellowship International
11300 Hampshire Avenue South
Minneapolis, Minnesota 55438

Printed in the United States of America by
Bethany Press International, Minneapolis, Minnesota 55438

Library of Congress Cataloging-in-Publication Data

Rue, Nancy N.
    The hostage / Nancy Rue.
        p.   cm. — (The Christian heritage series, the Charleston years ;
bk. 5)
    Summary: While tensions between the North and the South gradually
increase all around him, eleven-year-old Austin faces troubles of his own as a
hostage in pre-Civil War Charleston.
    ISBN 1–56179–638–7
    [1. Slavery—Fiction.   2. Charleston (S.C.)—History—1775–1865—
Fiction.   3. Christian life—Fiction.]   I. Title.   II. Series: Rue, Nancy N.
Christian heritage series, the Charleston Years ; bk. 5.
PZ7.R88515Ho   1998
[Fic]—dc21   98–25553
                                                                      CIP
                                                                      AC

98 99 00 01 02/10 9 8 7 6 5 4 3 2 1

For Barbara Dirks,
who has passed through
many a narrow gate

A Map of
Charleston
1860-1861

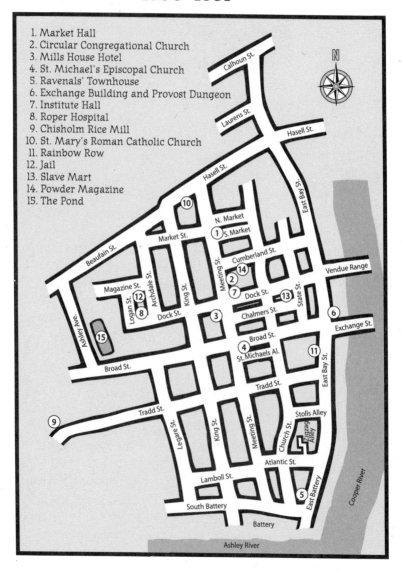

1. Market Hall
2. Circular Congregational Church
3. Mills House Hotel
4. St. Michael's Episcopal Church
5. Ravenals' Townhouse
6. Exchange Building and Provost Dungeon
7. Institute Hall
8. Roper Hospital
9. Chisholm Rice Mill
10. St. Mary's Roman Catholic Church
11. Rainbow Row
12. Jail
13. Slave Mart
14. Powder Magazine
15. The Pond

Chapter One

"**M**assa Austin, where you *been?*"

Austin Hutchinson hung on to the Charleston Harbor pier railing and tried to catch his breath as he grinned up into the scowling face of the slave boy.

"I was just down there looking at that cotton shipment, Henry-James," Austin said. He held up a scratched hand. "Did you know the leaves on that stuff are so spiny that they'll cut you up? Lucky for you Uncle Drayton grows rice."

Henry-James pulled his lips into a thick line. "Lucky for you I don't tell him you done run off without tellin' nobody where you was goin'."

"You don't have to look after me," Austin said.

He tried to straighten his 11-year-old self up to Henry-James's 13-year-old height. He was unsuccessful, of course. Even if he had been five feet six inches tall like his friend, Austin would have felt smaller. Henry-James seemed as big as life itself sometimes.

Right now he was still frowning down at Austin. "I do so got to look after you, Massa Austin. I ain't never knowed a boy could get hisself into so much trouble without even *tryin'*." He squinted his dark eyes suspiciously. "You wasn't talkin' to nobody, was you? It's your mouth what gets you into them messes."

1

"What messes?" said another voice behind them. "Are you in a mess again, Austin?"

It was Austin's 11-year-old cousin, Charlotte Ravenal. She climbed to the bottom rung of the pier railing, green cape blowing out behind her in the harbor wind, and looked at Austin with her golden eyes, the same color as his, shining like honey in the December sun.

"You would think I did nothing but get myself into trouble," Austin said.

He tried to glare at them, but it was hard. In the first place, they were right. He did seem to be in one scrape or another most of the time. And in the second place, they were the two best friends he'd made since he and his mother and his little brother, Jefferson, had come to South Carolina to stay on his Uncle Drayton's Canaan Grove plantation near Charleston last January. It was hard to stay mad at them for longer than a minute or two. He cut it off at 15 seconds this time and grinned again.

Charlotte smiled back, wrinkling the freckles that dotted her nose just the way Austin's did his nose. As a matter of fact, most things about them were the same, except that Charlotte's long, acorn-colored hair flowed down over her shoulders, while Austin's was trimmed close around his ears and fell in wisps across his forehead.

Henry-James gave one more scowl and then slung two more bags of rice over his shoulder and carried them off to the gangplank that led to the expectant ship.

"So did you talk to anyone?" Charlotte said to Austin.

"Believe it or not," Austin said, "I didn't talk. I listened."

Charlotte's eyes lit up, and she moved closer. "And what did you hear?"

Now Austin did frown. "Bad things," he said. "Those cotton growers—" he pointed down the dock toward them "—they're saying that some kind of Vigilance Committees have been formed to make sure the slaves don't have any meetings or even talk to each other in groups. They said ever since Abraham Lincoln was elected, they've been getting more and more scared that there's going to be a slave uprising."

Charlotte's smile faded, and she bit at her lip. "What does *vigilance* mean, Boston?" she said.

When she used his nickname—short for Boston Austin—he knew she was hoping he had the answer. And he did, of course. There weren't many words Austin Hutchinson didn't understand.

"That means they're going to be watching the slaves like a bunch of hawks," he said. "And they don't care about the law— they're taking the law into their own hands. That's what they said."

"We have to tell Henry-James and Daddy Elias," Charlotte said solemnly. "They can't have any more prayer meetings."

"They have to have meetings, Lottie!" Austin said, backbone stiffening. "We just have to warn them to be careful."

Charlotte folded her arms across her chest, suddenly shivering in the brisk air. "No, Austin," she said. "You know if Henry-James gets in any trouble at all, Daddy will sell him sure enough. You were there when he tried it before!"

Austin knew she was right. And he knew something else, too—that Henry-James and Kady, Austin's oldest cousin, had a secret they wouldn't tell him. That surely smacked of trouble.

But Austin shook his head firmly. "Uncle Drayton's changed his mind about a lot of things since then," he said. "He let Henry-James learn to read. He doesn't believe in South Carolina seceding from the Union."

"Did I hear my name over here?"

Both Austin and Charlotte whirled around to see a tall figure coming toward them enveloped in a dark blue greatcoat that flapped out from his trim suit. With his cheeks ruddy from the cold sea air and his posture erect with the business at hand, he looked handsome and in charge. Austin thought what he always did when his uncle looked like that—that he would like to look the same someday. He was already halfway there, since they had the same hair, the same eyes, the same turned-up Ravenal nose that even his mother, Sally, had.

But Uncle Drayton didn't look like that too often these days. The more the South talked of secession, the more cloudy-eyed he became, the more he locked himself in his library, and the more he seemed to drift away while his wife, Aunt Olivia, and his second daughter, Polly, were babbling about the upcoming social season. At least right now, as he ordered his thousands of bushels of rice onto the ship, he had that bright, alive look again.

"Were y'all talking about me?" Uncle Drayton said as he reached them and put a hand on each of their shoulders.

"Well, actually," Austin said, "we were talking about the Vigilance Committees."

Charlotte gave him one of her you'll-never-learn-to-hush-up looks, but Austin just focused on Uncle Drayton with a cocked head.

"I don't know why they're wasting their time," Uncle Drayton said. "I don't want a slave uprising either, heaven knows, but far as I can tell, my slaves have been too busy gathering the food crops and getting the rice ready for shipping—not to mention repairing all the dikes for the next planting. I don't see when they'd have time to plan a mutiny, do you?"

Charlotte shook her head violently and signaled Austin with her eyes to do the same. But he only gnawed on his mouth for a moment before he said, "Do you really think there's going to be a war, Uncle Drayton?"

Uncle Drayton let his hands slip off their shoulders, and his face drew in tight and thoughtful. Charlotte sighed a there-is-no-stopping-you-Austin sigh.

"If those Fire Eaters who are meeting right now decide that

South Carolina should break away from the Union, there surely will be a war," Uncle Drayton said. "And it's entirely unnecessary. But people aren't asking me, are they?"

He gave a smile Austin could tell he didn't feel and stepped away from them, his eyes back on the masts that poked up in bunches along the wharf, his feet maneuvering quickly among the bundles of cotton and the barrels of turpentine and rosin that waited to be loaded onto ships.

Austin knew why he was suddenly sad again. His uncle had been a loyal, respected citizen of South Carolina all his life, but when he didn't agree to secession, most of his old friends had turned on him. No one had invited him to be a part of the decision-making conference.

"Uh-oh," Charlotte said.

"What?" Austin said.

He followed her pointing finger with his eyes and at once felt a sizzle of anxiety in his chest. Two men stalked toward them, one tall and long-legged with eyebrows like caterpillars that met in the middle when he was angry, the other short and stout with side whiskers that stuck out from his cheeks like bear fur. When he got excited, he flared his nostrils and wheezed, donkey-style. He was doing both now as they drew near, their eyes firing at Uncle Drayton.

"Ravenal!" gasped the short one, Lawson Chesnut. "A word with you, please, sir!"

The tall man, Virgil Rhett, drew his eyebrows together and nodded sharply. Uncle Drayton stopped, turned, and glowered at them. Lawson Chesnut showed his yellow teeth like an aggressive dog but stopped out of Uncle Drayton's reach and rocked back on his heels with his hands clasped over his belly.

His fingers can hardly touch, Austin thought. *He's just a fat old bagpipe of a thing.*

The bagpipe at once began to bellow.

"I see you've had a fine crop this year, Mr. Ravenal," Lawson Chesnut said. "What did you yield, 40 bushels to the acre?"

"Sixty-five," Uncle Drayton said stiffly.

Austin sidled closer to Charlotte and tried to make himself invisible. Usually they were sent away just when the conversation got interesting, and he really wanted to hear this.

"Impressive," Chesnut said. He nodded to Virgil Rhett, who nodded back. "With your thousand acres of rice fields, that comes to quite a tidy sum."

"I'm proud of it," Uncle Drayton said. He narrowed his eyes. "But I doubt you came all the way out here to congratulate me on my good fortune. What is it, gentlemen? I have work to do."

"Well, we did have a question," Lawson Chesnut said, once again looking to Virgil Rhett for a nod. They were beginning to make Austin feel seasick.

"Then ask it," Uncle Drayton said. After all that had happened with these two men and their other "Fire Eating" secessionist friends, Austin was sure it was all Uncle Drayton could do not to shove the two of them right into the harbor. His eyes were smoldering, and there was none of the usual honey and molasses in his voice.

Chesnut flashed his yellow teeth again. "We were simply wondering, Mr. Ravenal, how you expect to continue to produce rice so successfully without slaves."

Uncle Drayton's eyebrows shot up, and he looked behind him at Henry-James and Isaac and the swarm of other black men who were hoisting bags up onto their backs.

"I have no intention of even trying it without slaves," he said. "As you see, I have 50 of them with me today."

"But Mr. Ravenal," Virgil Rhett said, eyebrows colliding, "with Abraham Lincoln in office, slavery will soon be a thing of the past. People who were foreordained by God to be our servants will be freed, and we will be left with nothing."

Uncle Drayton sighed wearily. "We have had this conversation before, gentlemen," he said. "Lincoln has not said he would free the slaves we already have. He even went so far as to say that slavery will probably disappear on its own eventually, so why disturb—?"

"He's a liar!" Chesnut shouted. His thick face turned as dark as a blueberry. If Austin hadn't had that sizzle of fear in his chest, he would have nudged Charlotte to make sure she saw how ridiculous he looked.

"He'll order us to let our slaves go the minute he's inaugurated!" Virgil Rhett said. "That is why we must break away from the Union before it comes to that."

Uncle Drayton shook his head. "You're asking for war if you do that. You don't think the government is just going to let us walk away and form our own little country, do you?"

Chesnut gave a laugh that sounded for all the world like a snort. He swept his arm out over the harbor, hiking up his jacket comically. "So let there be war," he said. "We'll win it in a day with all that."

Austin looked to where Chesnut was wildly gesturing. From where they stood, they could see four forts in the harbor—Fort Johnson on James Island, Fort Moultrie on Sullivan's Island, Castle Pinckney, and Fort Sumter. To Austin, they looked like big stone playhouses whose only attackers at the moment were seabirds—a few osprey and a couple of cormorants.

"I would prefer not to have any fighting at all," Uncle Drayton said coldly. "The thought of cannon fire does not excite me, as it obviously does you."

"I am excited by freedom!" Lawson Chesnut said, gasping for air.

Virgil Rhett wiped that away with his hand. "That is neither here nor there," he said. "We have come to warn you, Ravenal."

"Again?" Uncle Drayton said, his voice still cool. "What is your empty threat this time?"

"I wouldn't call it empty," Chesnut said. He nodded smugly at Virgil, who, of course, nodded back. "Those Vigilance Committees I'm sure you've heard about—"

Austin elbowed Charlotte.

"—they aren't just for those conniving slaves. They're to catch anyone who doesn't stand behind the cause of secession and independence for the South." Chesnut leaned in—as far as he could over his bulging stomach. "And that includes abolitionists."

"What do I have to say to you to get it through that thick head of yours, Chesnut?" Uncle Drayton said angrily. "I am not an abolitionist!"

"But you have them living right under your roof! That's just as bad, to hear the Vigilantes tell it."

Virgil pointed a long finger at Uncle Drayton's nose. "Don't say we didn't warn you, Ravenal," he said. "And if something awful happens to your family, don't claim you didn't bring it on yourself."

"I've told you this before," Chesnut cut in with a wheeze, "if you aren't with us, you're against us."

"Get those abolitionists out of your house," Virgil Rhett said. "Come around to secession, support independence. . . ."

Any other time, Austin would have whispered to Charlotte that the man sounded like he was reciting a lesson in school. But the sizzle of anxiety had fanned up to full-blown fear in his chest. All he could do was remain still and hope they'd go away without noticing him.

After all, the abolitionists living under Uncle Drayton's roof were, of course, his mother, his little brother, and Austin himself. The very reason they were staying at Canaan Grove was because his mother was too sickly to travel anymore, and his father was continuing his mission to spread the word of antislavery through his lectures and pamphlets.

Charlotte silently curled her fingers around Austin's wrist and squeezed until Rhett and Chesnut turned importantly on their heels and tapped off down the dock with Uncle Drayton searing their backs with his eyes. Only when they'd disappeared inside their carriage did anyone breathe. Austin let his air out in a *whoosh* that resounded across the water.

"That was close," he said. "I was sure they were going to see me and—"

"They're only trying to scare me," Uncle Drayton said. He smiled at them crisply—another smile that didn't reach his eyes—and dusted off his hands. "We're all but finished here. Suppose you two climb into the carriage and we'll go to the hotel for dinner."

"The Mills House?" Charlotte said.

"Nowhere but, sweet thing," Uncle Drayton said. "Run on, now."

"I love the scalloped oysters they serve there," Charlotte said as Uncle Drayton hurried back toward the ship and they headed toward one of Uncle Drayton's green broughams. "I can almost taste them."

"Do you think he's right?" Austin said.

"Who, Daddy? About what?"

"About us being safe from the Vigilantes. Do you think they really are just trying to scare him into joining them?"

Charlotte climbed up onto the carriage step and twisted a strand of her hair, the way she always did when she was thinking. "Daddy has stood up to them for months now," she said finally. "I think he knows what he's doing."

"Hmmm," Austin said.

Charlotte poked him in the side with her finger. "Boston," she said, "don't borrow trouble. We have Christmas coming up and then we're coming to Charleston for the social season. Let's just have fun."

Austin glanced at her sideways as she yanked him by the arm into the carriage. "You might convince me," he said, "if you tell me again about Christmas at Canaan Grove."

Charlotte at once spilled out a delightful sampling of Christmas traditions, everything from the pile of new toys they could expect to the turkey and plum pudding that would appear on the table. Austin soaked it all in as Uncle Drayton joined them, and with Henry-James at the reins they lurched in the carriage down rutted Market Street. It was choked with merchants and hawkers all trying to sell their wares. Henry-James had to stop lest they run over the women hauling their cartloads of potatoes and beets.

"What's going on out there?" Uncle Drayton said, peering out the window.

The only answer he got was a chorus of shouts from the street.

"Red rose to-may-toes!"

"Green peas! Green peas! Sweet as sugar—green peas!"

"Jui-cee lemons! Come and get 'em! Jui-cee lemons!"

"This is making me hungry," Austin said.

"Oooh, smell that?" Charlotte said. She closed her eyes and sniffed. "That's the Waffle Man."

"Get 'em hot, piping hot!" came the cry from outside. "Waffles here!"

And then from amid the shouts of the sellers, a harsh voice slashed through, like a blade that cut the life out of the market.

"You're a traitor to your homeland, you miserable cur!"

"No. Slaves, listen, all of you!" another voice cried above it. "Put down your plows and your serving trays and your horse-and-buggy reins! Be free! You have the right to be free!"

"Good heavens!" Uncle Drayton said.

He pried open the carriage door and stepped out into the clogged street. Charlotte and Austin crowded into the doorway behind him, but he held up a hand to keep them from coming any farther.

Market Street was becoming a mob scene. Two men—one of whom Austin recognized as Roger Pryor, another of the Fire Eaters—were struggling to drag a kicking, red-faced man up onto a wooden platform reserved for merchants. A man with a basket of collards and greens willingly let them take it over.

"What's happening?" Austin said.

"They've caught themselves an abolitionist," Uncle Drayton said.

"There is a law here that says we have the right to own slaves!" Roger Pryor cried out in his nasal voice. He tossed his long hair with a jerk of his head.

"We should be obeying a higher law!" the red-faced abolitionist shouted back. "God's law is above the Constitution! Any law that guarantees liberty and justice to the nation's people and then allows them to own and mistreat each other is wrong!"

"Slaves are not people—they're property!" Roger Pryor said, once again snapping his hair back. "The Bible has proof of it, if you want higher law!"

Only the restraint of Charlotte holding his arm reminded Austin *not* to raise it in anger, *not* to scream back at them.

Henry-James is not property! he wanted to cry. *And neither is Ria or Daddy Elias or Isaac or Tot—they're people! Better people than you!*

"And you're no better than a slave, coming in here and stirring up trouble!" Roger Pryor shouted at the struggling man. He pointed his long nose at the crowd, which grumbled in hostile fashion in front of him. "What do you say we do with him?"

"Tar and feather him!" someone cried.

The crowd seemed to like that idea. They gave an ugly cheer and even pressed forward as if they were all going to take the man to the tar pit like one giant executioner.

"What does tar and feather mean?" Charlotte asked.

"Just what it sounds like," Austin said. "They'll dip him in tar and then cover him with feathers."

"That's horrible!" Charlotte said.

"Back inside, both of you," Uncle Drayton said. "Henry-James, get us out of here."

"Yessir," Henry-James said from his seat atop the carriage.

"Do you want me to go up there with him and help?" Austin said.

He was already halfway out of the carriage. Uncle Drayton grabbed his arm to shove him back inside, but he was too late. Someone else took hold of Uncle Drayton's greatcoat from behind and pulled him backward. Austin was suddenly nose to nose with Virgil Rhett.

"Here's another one!" Rhett shouted to the crowd.

A few people at the back of the mob turned around to stare.

"He's just a boy!" someone shouted.

"All the more reason—stop it while he's young!" cried Lawson Chesnut from somewhere.

There were shouts of "Yes, do it!" and Austin heard no one disagreeing—except Uncle Drayton, who yanked himself away from whoever was restraining him and clawed both his hands into the backs of Virgil Rhett's shoulders.

"You leave that boy alone!" Uncle Drayton cried. With a jerk, he flung Rhett down.

"He's Drayton Ravenal's nephew!" Rhett screeched as he hit the ground. "He's Wesley Hutchinson's son!"

The stragglers at the back of the crowd gave a unanimous growl and began to move in like a large badger.

"Get inside, Austin!" Uncle Drayton shouted at him.

But before Austin could move, something hard and foul hit him squarely on the cheek and broke open with a splat.

‡ ‑ ❧ ‑ ‡

verything sped up into a whirling frenzy then.

Charlotte screamed. Uncle Drayton shoved Austin into the carriage, hauled himself in, and slammed the door. The carriage pitched forward, and outside there were terrified shrieks and angry shouts as Henry-James drove the horses right through the mass of mob members and merchants.

Inside the carriage, Austin slumped in the seat, too afraid to put his hand up to his throbbing cheek to see what had been hurled at him. Uncle Drayton pulled out a silk handkerchief and wiped it across Austin's face. A foul odor assaulted all their nostrils.

"Ugh! What *is* that?" Charlotte asked, freckled nose wrinkling.

"A rotten apple," Uncle Drayton said. "Probably more insulting than hurtful."

Austin nodded.

"It's still just a scare tactic," Uncle Drayton said. "Don't you worry now." But just the same, he pulled open the tiny window that divided them from Henry-James and said briskly, "On to the boat, Henry-James. We're going to head back to Canaan Grove."

It was a quiet trip back up the Ashley River on Uncle Drayton's packet boat. There was no talk of Christmas celebrations. There only seemed to be silent thoughts about tarring and feathering and rotten apples. Austin was glad when a few hours later the green velvety steps of the Canaan Grove terrace came into sight. He was even happy to see 7-year-old Jefferson tearing down them to meet the boat, especially since he had Henry-James's bloodhoundish mutt Bogie at his heels. They both howled until Charlotte, Austin, and Henry-James were off the boat.

Bogie's wrinkled skin flopped back and forth as he jumped up and put both paws on Austin's shoulders.

"You should be glad you didn't come with us, Bogie," Austin said to him. "It was ugly in town."

"Can we play now?" Jefferson said. "It's so boring when you're gone."

"Not now, little man," Uncle Drayton said as he marched up the hill toward the Big House. "I want everyone in the drawing room at once. We'll have dinner there. Henry-James, lay out a change of clothes for me for later and see to a fire in the library."

As Uncle Drayton's body slave, Henry-James was required to tend to all his personal needs, everything from bringing him his coffee before he got out of bed to shining his boots and taking care of his hunting hounds. That always made Jefferson's blue eyes stormy. He thought Henry-James should be seeing to *his* needs—which had mostly to do with playing, playing, and more playing.

"Come on, shrimp," Austin said to him. "You heard Uncle Drayton."

Jefferson followed, sniffing the air. "What's that smell?" he said.

That was the main topic of conversation the minute Austin walked into the drawing room. When he leaned over to hug his mother, who was propped up on pillows on the settee, she looked at him curiously and said, "Honey, have you stepped in something?"

His 14-year-old cousin Polly was less polite. She took one whiff from her place on the chaise longue, where her faithful slave girl, Tot, stood behind her as always, and said loudly, "What is that horrible stench?"

Jefferson tossed his dark curls and pointed a chubby finger. "It's Austin," he said.

"It's not *me*," Austin said. "It's the rotten apple somebody threw at me."

Aunt Olivia, who was standing in the doorway greeting her husband, at once thrust out a dimpled hand, and her slave, Mousie, put an ever-ready handkerchief into it. She placed it over her mouth and nose, though Austin could still see her wobbling double chins. They always fascinated Austin. They seemed to hang down as loosely as the dark brown ringlets she arranged on her head.

Polly, too, put out her hand for a hanky, but Tot couldn't seem to find one. She finally plucked up the corner of her starched apron and stuck it over Polly's nose. Polly pushed it away, sending her listless reddish curls jittering. Polly, Austin had noticed lately, wasn't quite as homely as she used to be, but at the moment, with her face contorted to ward off the apple odor, she reminded him of a disgruntled owl.

"Rotten apple?" Kady said. She had turned from the desk in the corner and was surveying Austin with interest. Besides Charlotte, Kady was his favorite cousin. Not only was she handsome with her dark shiny hair that was never fussy and her sympathetic, honey-colored eyes, but she was witty and fun. Plus, she believed so many of the same things Austin and his mother believed. Those were the very things that made it hard for her to live in her own home anymore. At 17, she couldn't just leave, unless she were married. And she had already proven to her parents last fall that she wasn't about to do that.

"Someone threw a rotten apple at him when we were passing

through the market," Uncle Drayton said. "Let's all sit down, shall we?"

Sally Hutchinson was at once on the edge of her seat. Beside her, Ria, Henry-James's mother and Sally's nurse, came to an attention so stiff the bones on her thin face seemed to stick out.

"Someone threw something at Austin?" Mother said. "Why on earth, Drayton?"

"Because they recognized him as an abolitionist's son," Uncle Drayton said. "The Fire Eaters have gone crazy out there."

Mother made Austin go over to Ria to be examined, which he endured reluctantly. He was never sure whether Ria approved of him. She said he put dangerous ideas into Henry-James's head.

While he stood there under the pressure of Ria's probing fingers, the conversation buzzed around him.

"What does that mean?" Mother said. "Will they come after him?"

"Come after *him?*" Aunt Olivia said with a hand to her chest. "What about *us?*"

"Daddy, you don't really think we're in danger, do you?" Kady chimed in.

"Danger?" Polly cried. "What kind of danger?"

And then as if she suspected the worst, she grabbed on to Tot's arm with both birdlike hands and hung on.

"If everyone would just calm down," Uncle Drayton said wearily, "I will explain." He looked toward the door where Josephine and two little slaves were waiting with steaming trays. "Come," he said to them. "Let's get everyone fed so we can all think like sane people."

But although everyone was presented with a bowl of okra stew thick with corn, tomatoes, onions, and lima beans and poured over rice, no one seemed interested in eating. Jefferson did pay attention to his bowl, but only to pick out the onions, each of which he regarded with a curled-up lip.

"Drayton, really," Austin's mother said to her brother, "how serious is it? Are they going to limit themselves to throwing smelly food at young boys—or is there more we need to worry about?"

"Isn't that serious enough?" Aunt Olivia said before Uncle Drayton could answer. "I certainly don't want things thrown at my children, especially when we go to Charleston for the social season."

She looked at Uncle Drayton, who stayed silent. Aunt Olivia began to blink rapidly. "We are going, Drayton, aren't we? We missed it last year because Sally and the boys arrived. I won't spend another year being left out of things!"

"Mama," Kady said, "as much as I want to go to Charleston, too, I really think safety is a little more important than whether you miss a few parties."

Aunt Olivia drew herself up haughtily. "Those parties are my life, Kady Sarah—a life you, of course, have chosen not to participate in, despite the fact that I sent you to Charleston for French lessons, paid hundreds for your wardrobe—"

"I want to participate!" Polly said. She turned her stricken face toward her father. "I'm 14 now!" she whined. "This is the first year I'm allowed to go to some of the parties, Daddy! You aren't going to let this stop us, are you?"

Austin felt a little stung. If Polly had said that two months ago, it wouldn't have surprised him. But he'd thought they were starting to be friends. He tried to shrug it off. *I guess you really learn who your friends are when it gets down to the important things*, he thought.

He looked at Charlotte. Now *there* was a friend. Her face was so pale that her freckles stood out like little flecks of pepper. She was as scared as he was about where this discussion was going.

"I am concerned for *everyone's* safety," Austin's mother said.

"I've been protecting you all quite well, haven't I?" Uncle Drayton said.

"Of course you have. But until now, no one was attacking us. You've said it yourself—there's talk of war, and if that happens, we will be the enemy."

Jefferson's curly head came up from his bowl, his chin dripping with juice. "Who's the enemy?" he said. "Us?"

"Yes, you!" Aunt Olivia said. Her chins were wobbling at twice their normal rate, and her eyes were wild. "I know my opinion doesn't count for much with you, Drayton, but as for me, I wish you would send for Wesley at once to come and take his family back up north."

Austin jumped like a startled cat. "No! I don't want to run away! They can throw things at me all day—I don't care. I'm not afraid of them!"

"You will be when it's a shotgun aimed at you!" Aunt Olivia said. Then she waved her hand for her handkerchief again, as if she were about to faint at the very thought of it.

Polly squealed and buried her face in Tot's sleeve.

"I admire your bravery, Austin," Uncle Drayton said. "But your aunt is partly right. I think that rotten apple may be just a hint of things to come."

"But you said yourself in the carriage that they were only trying to scare you!" Austin said.

"I've had a little time to think about it since then," Uncle Drayton said. "And I still need more time. What I want to tell you while I have you all together is to take caution."

"What do you mean?" Polly said, peeking out from the folds of Tot's blue plaid dress.

"Do not go anywhere on the plantation alone. Keep your shutters closed, and do not go near the windows."

"Why?" Austin said.

"Because I say so," Uncle Drayton said abruptly. His voice was growing snappish, and his face looked pinched.

Still, Austin had to bite down on his lip to keep from persisting. What was wrong with being near the windows?

"We will keep our distance here until things settle down in Charleston, and then we shall see what happens."

"Are you saying we will not go to Charleston for the season?" Aunt Olivia said.

"I am not saying one way or the other," Uncle Drayton said. "I need time to think and to wait and see."

Aunt Olivia sniffed and daintily pushed her bowl away from her.

She's going to starve herself until she gets her way, Austin thought. *It couldn't hurt. She's getting awfully plump.*

He mentally shook himself. It was hard not to think ugly thoughts when someone was being so rude. But Daddy Elias wouldn't like him thinking that way. Henry-James's grandfather had taught him a lot about how to be a person Jesus would be proud to know. He was sure Jesus had never thought Mary Magdalene or any of the others were fat and hateful.

"Daddy," Polly said in a quavery voice, "I want a bodyguard. Will you station one of the slaves outside my door tonight while I sleep?"

Behind her, Tot nodded her head enthusiastically.

"I don't think that will be necessary, Pumpkin Polly," Uncle Drayton said.

"Why not? You've come in here and scared us all to death with your stories!" Aunt Olivia said. "If it will make the child feel safe—"

"Fine," Uncle Drayton said. "I'll have Henry-James do it."

Austin grinned for the first time since they'd left Charleston, and Charlotte grinned back. He knew what she was thinking. As soon as Polly was asleep, the three of them could have a secret meeting. With Henry-James working so much these days, it was hard to find time to spend with him.

"Do you want a bodyguard, too, Kadydid?" Uncle Drayton said.

Kady shook her shiny head. "No, thank you, Daddy. I don't think I have anything to fear from a bunch of scalawags."

Uncle Drayton's eyebrows shifted. "This isn't a band of ruffians," he said. "Though they pretend they aren't involved, we are talking about influential men who have long been respected in South Carolina." He tightened his lips. "That's what worries me. The people of this state have nothing to do with all this. It's a small group of powerful politicians who are behind it, seeing something in it for themselves."

"Then surely we have nothing to be afraid of," Aunt Olivia said, lips pursed. "A southern gentleman would never do anything dreadful. We have a code of honor in the South."

Code of honor or not, when Austin crawled into bed that night to wait for Jefferson to fall asleep, he heard the sound of shutters closing in the rooms up and down the hall. He looked up at the pale, wintry moon he could see through his window.

I'm not closing mine, he thought stubbornly. *That's like running away—and I won't do it.*

But he grunted to himself. It didn't matter what he said he would or wouldn't do—it was up to Uncle Drayton and his mother and even his father. If they said it was too dangerous to stay here, there would be nothing he could do to change that.

And he wanted to stay so badly. All his life he'd been traveling with his parents, living in hotel rooms and train cars. He'd never had a chance to make friends or have adventures until he came here. It had been hard at first. He was so different from his southern cousins and their slaves. But now this was home, and no matter how much he sometimes missed his father, it was the only real home he'd ever had.

He lay still now and listened to Jefferson's breathing. It was heavy and even; he was deep in his dreams. As stealthy as a robber, Austin crept out of bed and tiptoed to the door, where he peeked out into the hall. It was dark except for the occasional flicker from the socket lamp in the stairway, so he had to squint hard to see the shadowy figure squatting outside Polly's door. It was Charlotte, and Austin saw her motioning him out.

He padded silently down the hall and folded his lanky limbs down beside her.

"Where's Henry-James?" he whispered.

"I don't know," she whispered back. "When I first peeked out, he was right here, but by the time I got my dressing gown on and came out, he was gone." She put an embarrassed hand up to her mouth. "Maybe he had to go down to the . . . you know, the necessary."

Austin jerked his head toward the door. "Is Polly asleep yet?"

Charlotte grinned and nodded. "I heard her snoring a minute ago. She'd never admit it, but she snores like a train all night long."

"And she thinks somebody's going to marry her," Austin said. "We should warn whoever proposes."

"No," Charlotte said, eyes dancing. "I can't wait for her to get married. She makes me crazy!"

Austin opened his mouth for a laugh, but it never came out.

Instead there was a hard, shattering sound, followed by a prolonged round of smashing and splintering that all but ripped Austin's heart in two. And above it all, there was a terrified wail. It came from the direction of Austin's bedroom.

"Jefferson!" Austin cried.

The hall was suddenly alive with the screams and cries of Ravenals and Hutchinsons, all in their night clothes, their sleepy faces shocked and confused. Henry-James was the last to appear, right on Kady's heels.

"What was that?" someone said.

"It came from the boys' room!"

"What got broken?"

They all gathered around the doorway, but Uncle Drayton held up a commanding hand. "Stay back, all of you!" he said.

Austin had to cling to the door frame to keep from disobeying him. Jefferson was in there, and something big and hard had broken glass—right where his little brother was sleeping.

It seemed like forever before Uncle Drayton emerged, carrying a white-faced and trembling Jefferson. The little boy looked around wildly and held his arms out to his mother.

"What happened?" Kady said.

Austin didn't wait for an answer. He wriggled between Polly and Tot and saw for himself.

The window that overlooked the plantation had been shattered, and halfway across the room lay the culprit—a large rock with a piece of paper wrapped around it and tied on with a string. Beyond were shards of glass, some as big and deadly looking as butcher knives. One was lying on the bed, in the very spot Austin had vacated only a few minutes before.

Austin tried not to shudder. He quickly picked up the rock and went out the door. It was better not to think about the things that might have been.

By now Jefferson was calm in his mother's arms and was regaling them all with a story of seeing the glass come flying toward him, which couldn't possibly be true.

"What broke the window?" Kady said.

"This," Austin said. He held up the rock, and Uncle Drayton snatched it away. Austin felt Charlotte edge closer to him as Uncle Drayton untied the string and pulled off the paper.

"Does it say anything?" Polly said.

Uncle Drayton stared at the paper and looked for all the world as if he wanted to say no. But words were visible through the thin parchment, and Austin could even make out a few of them. One was "suffer." Another was "allegiance."

"It's nothing," Uncle Drayton said. He began to fold the paper with brisk fingers. "It's just a prank."

"If it's a prank, why are you keeping it?" Kady said.

"Drayton, don't you dare try to hide something from us," Austin's mother said. "I want the truth. This is about us, too."

Uncle Drayton sighed again. To Austin, he sounded more tired every time he did it.

"Take Jefferson into his mother's room, Tot," he said.

Jefferson let out a loud protest, but they were all used to that. It faded unnoticed behind Mother's closed door as Uncle Drayton reopened the note.

" 'Dear Mr. Ravenal,' " he read. " 'Your nephews will suffer if you don't send them back where they belong, and if you do not decide where your allegiance is.' "

"What does 'allegiance' mean?" Polly said, narrowing her eyes as if it were an ugly word.

"It means the duty a man feels he owes to his government," Uncle Drayton said. "They're asking me to decide whether I will be loyal to the Union or to the South, and I don't know that yet." He looked firmly at Mother. "But I do know one thing, Sally. You and the boys cannot stay here. I was wrong—these men are serious. And they won't stop until someone gets hurt. I can't protect you here."

"It's my fault!" Austin cried. "I left the shutters open!"

"Oh, don't be ridiculous!" Aunt Olivia said. "They would have found a way, and they will continue to. I think Drayton is right— you must all go!"

She's been wanting that ever since we got here, Austin thought. He swallowed angrily against the lump that was already forming in his throat. *What happened to southern gentlemen never behaving like ruffians?*

Austin looked at his mother, begging her with his eyes. But

Sally Hutchinson was nodding sadly. "I'm afraid you're right, Drayton," she said. "What if Austin had been in bed? He'd very likely have been killed."

"No, I wouldn't!"

"Maybe not this time," Aunt Olivia said. Austin could almost see her imagining his death, and enjoying it.

"We're going to have to leave," Mother said. She put out an arm to pull in Austin, but he shrank back against the wall.

"I'm sorry, son," she said. "But it's for our safety and everyone else's."

She looked back at Uncle Drayton, her eyes big in her paler-than-ever face. "What do we do?" she said.

"Let's go down to the library and draft a letter to Wesley," he said.

✝ ✦ ✝

Chapter Three

*A*ustin stayed in his mother's room while she went downstairs with Uncle Drayton. Jefferson slept in the middle of the four-poster rice bed, and Austin sat on one of Aunt Olivia's brocade chairs and stared at the photograph on the table.

His father's face stared back at him. Wesley Hutchinson looked like a grown-up Jefferson with his curvy, dark hair and big, blue eyes. But he was a serious man, always thinking about the cause of freedom for the slaves. As Austin looked at his solemn face, the thoughts went back and forth in his head like a seesaw.

He's a person Jesus would be proud to know, that's for sure.

I want to see him. I want him to see that I'm, maybe, that kind of person, too. But am I? He'd never run away like a scared cat—and that's what we're doing, it seems to me.

And I'm not ready to! There's too much to do here! What about Kady and Henry-James's secret? Why was he with her tonight instead of us? I need to know that. And what about Charlotte? We have so many plans for what we're going to do in Charleston. And what about all I still have to learn from Daddy Elias?

He looked glumly at the picture and hoped his smart father

would come up with an answer for him—a way to have everything perfect.

But he knew that if Wesley Hutchinson could have spoken to him right then, he'd have told him things just weren't perfect in life.

"That's for sure," Austin muttered.

He went to bed with the unsettled feeling that comes with an unanswered question. The next morning, before breakfast or his lessons with Kady, he ran to the one person he knew who could answer it for him.

There was a thin trail of smoke coming from the chimney of the slave cabin that Henry-James shared with his mother and his grandfather. The outside shutters were closed against the mid-December dampness, which meant it would be dark inside except for the breakfast fire. But there was always something cheery and bright about the little cabin when Daddy Elias was there.

Austin was relieved to find him still in his creaky rocking chair by the fireplace, even though Henry-James and Ria had already left for their work. But he was surprised to see him wrapped in a blanket and still wearing a knitted sleeping cap.

"Aren't you going to be late?" Austin said uneasily. "Won't you get into trouble?"

"Ain't gonna be no late nor no early today, Massa Austin," the old man said, smiling out of his spoon-shaped mouth. "Ain't gonna be no nothin'. Ria, she say I got to stay right here in this cabin till I gets rid o' this cough."

Austin settled on the floor at his feet. "Is that all right with Uncle Drayton?"

"I don't reckon it would be if'n it weren't the slow time. Henry-James, he'll take care o' most things out there till I gets back on my feet." He smiled down at the plate in his lap. "And long as I keeps eatin' Ria's cookin', I be cured quicker'n you can think."

Austin looked curiously at the plate. Daddy Elias was having ashcakes made out of meal, salt, and water that Ria had probably covered with ashes in the fire early this morning until they were brown. They looked delicious to Austin—though he couldn't say the same for the other, slimy looking concoction next to them.

"Can I share some ashcakes and chitlins with you, Massa Austin?" Daddy Elias said.

"What are chitlins?" Austin said, nostrils quivering suspiciously.

"Ain't nothin' but the intestines o' hogs. Mighty tasty."

Austin tried not to gag. "No, thanks," he said. "I'm not hungry."

Daddy Elias sparkled his faded old eyes at him and picked up the broken piece of pottery on the edge of his plate to start eating with it. "If'n you don't want no breakfast, Massa Austin," he said, "then I reckon you got somethin' on your mind this mornin'."

"I have a question," Austin said.

"Mmmm-hmmm."

Austin wriggled himself up onto his knees. "Mother and Uncle Drayton—and Aunt Olivia, of course—they all think we aren't safe here anymore. They think we should have my father come and take us back to the North."

"That don't sound like a question to me," Daddy Elias said. "Sound like the decision already been made." He pushed a portion of the chitlins into his mouth and chewed thoughtfully.

"They don't have a question. I do," Austin said. "I wonder, isn't this like running away? Shouldn't we stay and stand up for what we believe in?"

"Now that sound real nice, Massa Austin," Daddy Elias said. "It sure do. But that standin' up for what you believes in—that ain't always easy."

Austin felt himself frown. "So you think we should take the easy way?"

Daddy Elias smiled so widely that Austin could see the ash-cake in his mouth. "No, sirree, I ain't sayin' nothin' like that," the old man said. "You just gots to know what it be like to go through that there narrow gate."

Austin forced himself not to sigh. *Here we go again,* he thought. *Daddy Elias always has to make it so hard to figure out. Why can't he just say what he means?*

"What narrow gate?" Austin said.

"That one you got to go through if'n you gonna do things right."

"I don't understand," Austin said impatiently. "And I don't have time to figure it out. They've already sent off a message to my father."

"Marse Jesus, He always get the truth to you in time, don't He?"

Daddy Elias watched him over the last of his chitlins and ash-cake. Austin watched back and thought.

He and "Marse Jesus" *had* become friends. Austin prayed to Him all the time, and he even sometimes felt as if He were right here beside him. Knowing the way Jesus would want him to do things had helped him more than once since he'd been at Canaan Grove.

Austin had to nod. "I guess so," he said. "But what do I do?"

"You got to watch for that there narrow gate," Daddy Elias said. "And then you gots to make sure you can get through it."

Austin wanted to ask a thousand questions about that. Where *was* this narrow gate? What did it look like? Was it going to hurt to go through it?

But Daddy Elias began to cough so hard that he had to set his plate aside and pull a yellowed handkerchief out of the pocket of his jeans pants. His shoulders shook violently from his hacking, and Austin was scared.

"Should I do something?" Austin called out over the coughing.

Daddy Elias pointed to a bowl on the stove that was covered with a towel. Austin grabbed it and brought it to him, and Daddy Elias dipped into the gooey stuff with his hand while he pulled open his shirt. Pushing aside a small bag on a string that hung around his neck, he rubbed the goo onto his skin, and slowly the cough subsided.

"What is that?" Austin said.

"That there is a flaxseed poultice Ria done fixed up for me," he said. "That take care of the new-mony while this here camphor on the string keep the chills and fever away." He gave a feeble smile as he handed the bowl to Austin and sank into the rocker.

Austin could hear his breath rattling all the way across the room as he took the bowl back to the stove.

"You're really sick, aren't you, Daddy Elias?" Austin said. "Pneumonia is serious."

Daddy Elias waved him off. "Ria, she just got to make a fuss, is all."

"No," Austin said, "you're sick. My mother's been sickly ever since I can remember. I know sick when I see it."

"Well, I's old, Massa Austin. Sick come with bein' old."

Austin felt strangely angry. "No!" he said. "You just need to be taken care of, that's all. Ria should be down here with you."

"She takin' care of your mama. Now that's more important."

"My mother is doing fine now," Austin said.

Daddy Elias shut his eyes and slowly shook his crusty head with its crinkly gray hair that covered the back half of his otherwise bald head. "All's I needs is for somebody to pour me some of that there rosemary tea Ria got brewin', and I'll be back in them fields in no time."

Austin poured the tea. He also stoked the fire and brought out another blanket from the bedroom and read Daddy Elias some verses from the Bible. Only when the old man nodded off in his chair did Austin tiptoe out and go back to the Big House.

I don't care what he says, Austin thought as he took the back steps two at a time. *I'm talking to Mother about this.*

But telling his mother anything was hard. The Big House was bustling with so much activity when he got inside that he couldn't even *find* his mother. Mousie told him she was somewhere, helping make the garlands.

"What garlands?" Austin said.

But Aunt Olivia screeched from the drawing room, and Mousie skittered off. Charlotte bounded out of the dining room, arms loaded with boxwood and crabapples, eyes sparkling.

"What's going on?" Austin said.

"We're getting ready for Christmas," she said. "You missed it at breakfast—Mama stood up and said she didn't care what those miserable people in Charleston were doing, she was going to have Christmas in her house. It's only six days away, and we have work to do."

"What's all that?" Austin said, pointing to the mound of greenery in Charlotte's arms.

"These are to make garlands," she said. "We're doing them in the music room—Kady and Aunt Sally and me." She took off across the hall, tossing her parting words over her shoulder. "You can help—or you can go out in the kitchen building and help Polly and Tot make tallow candles."

"No, thanks," Austin said, wrinkling his nose. He'd helped make tallow candles once—standing there while they boiled beef tripe and kidneys until the fat stewed down. He wasn't sure which was more disgusting, the smell or the way the tallow oozed into the molds while he held the string up straight.

"I just need to talk to my mother," he said.

But before he could even take three steps toward the music room, the library door flew open, and Uncle Drayton appeared in the doorway, white-faced and twitching. He waved a newspaper over his head. Austin knew it could only be the *Charleston Mercury*.

"Olivia! Sally!" he cried. "Come here! Come here at once!"

Charlotte dropped the whole armload of greenery on the floor, and doors all over the Big House flew open. Tot and Polly even heard in the kitchen building and bolted in through the back door. Austin felt the sizzle of fear in his chest again.

"Drayton, for heaven's sake, what *is* it?" Aunt Olivia said, bustling out into the hallway from the drawing room, chins a-wobble. "I am *trying* to figure out how much gingerbread—"

But at the sight of Uncle Drayton's pasty-white face, even Aunt Olivia stopped and thrust her pudgy hand to her chest. "What on earth?" she said shrilly. "What ever is the matter?"

Mother leaned on Kady's arm, her face as white as Uncle Drayton's. "Tell us, Drayton," she said. "You're frightening me."

For another moment, all Uncle Drayton could seem to do was wave the paper. Finally, he took a breath and said, "They're going to take the vote on secession on December 20. They're going to decide on our entire future tomorrow."

Polly put her hands on her skinny waist. "I don't see why they can't wait until after Christmas and the season. They're spoiling everything."

"Polly, you're such a pumpkin head," Kady said. "Don't you see? If they vote for secession, there's going to be a war with the northern states. Aunt Sally and Austin and Jefferson would be hauled in like prisoners."

"And what's to happen to you, Drayton?" Aunt Olivia said, still clutching her now-blotchy chest. "You've been against secession all this time. Won't they treat you like the enemy, too? And the rest of us?"

Her eyes appeared to Austin as if they were about to burst from her head. She was so upset that she even smacked away the handkerchief Mousie offered her.

"I don't know what it means yet," Uncle Drayton said. "I only know that I must be in Charleston when the vote is taken. I must know the minute it is decided. Otherwise, we're left at the mercy of those—" He stopped abruptly and folded the newspaper with a firm crease. "Get yourself ready to go with me, Olivia," he said. "You and the girls."

"What about us?" Austin said.

"I don't think it's safe," Uncle Drayton said. "Don't you agree, Sally?"

Austin's mother nodded. "We should wait here for word from Wesley."

"All right, then," Uncle Drayton said. "There is work to be done."

Chaos erupted in the hallway as everyone rushed to lay aside the Christmas preparations and start packing. Austin stood there with the sizzling fear turning to heavy disappointment in his chest.

You can't just leave me here! he wanted to shout at them all. *Just because I'm going away soon doesn't mean you can start leaving me out now!*

However, no one seemed interested in what Austin thought . . . or said . . . or did. They brushed past him and stepped around him until Polly finally said, "Boston, would you please *move* before you get run over? Tot is going to be dragging a hat box through here for me."

Miserably, Austin stepped aside and trudged slowly up the staircase. *I wish Daddy Elias had told me more than to look for the narrow gate*, he thought. *I don't think that's going to help me very much.*

By early the next morning, the packet boat was loaded with bags and baskets, ready to make the trip down the Ashley River to Charleston once more. Austin stood at the dock in the raw, gray cold and watched Henry-James carry Uncle Drayton's two big leather bags aboard. Mother and Jefferson were still in bed, and he felt terribly alone as the only Hutchinson in the midst of all the Ravenals. He was already feeling like an outsider.

"Uncle Drayton is taking a lot of things," Austin said. "How long are you going to be gone?"

Henry-James had to turn all the way around to see Austin because of the bags on his shoulders.

"Don't know, Massa Austin," he said. "Marse Drayton, he ain't talkin' much to nobody." He showed the gap between his two front teeth in a smile. "I'd a tol' you if'n I knew, don't you think?"

Austin wasn't sure. He'd started to go down to the slave cabin last night, but when he'd seen Henry-James and Kady whispering on the front porch, he'd turned around and come back to the Big House. Nothing was feeling quite the same.

"I wish you were going with us," said a voice behind him.

Charlotte came close, shivering near his elbow in spite of the thick, green cape wrapped around her.

"Don't you be givin' him no ideas, Miz Lottie," Henry-James said. His big, black eyes narrowed into slits. "Don't nobody need to be makin' no more trouble than we already got."

"Henry-James! Get those bags aboard!" Uncle Drayton trumpeted from the boat. "Charlotte, come on now! We're ready to go!"

Henry-James hurried on board. Charlotte pretended to, though she stopped as soon as her father disappeared inside the cabin and twisted her foot on the dock.

"I don't care what Henry-James says," she said. "I still wish you were going. What if Uncle Wesley comes for you while we're gone?"

Without meeting his eyes, she darted off toward the gangplank and vanished into the cabin's shadows. Austin looked hard at the ark-shaped boat with his heart pounding.

What if he does? he thought frantically. *I couldn't do it. I couldn't leave her and Henry-James without saying good-bye!*

Austin looked anxiously at the lower door that led to the crew's cuddy. Any minute, big-muscled Isaac would be coming out to pull up the gangplank and cast off. He took one last glance over his shoulder. The plantation was still half-asleep behind him. No one would miss him for hours. Mother would barely have time to work up a good worry before they would be back.

Uncle Drayton said he didn't think it was safe. He didn't say I couldn't go. Who knows, maybe this is the narrow gate Daddy Elias was talking about.

Austin hurried up the gangplank.

✝ ✦ ✝

Chapter Four

The boat's deck was the roof of the cabin. Austin scrambled up its ladder, only slipping once, and flattened himself onto the boards like one of Josephine's hotcakes. He didn't dare lift his head as he heard the cuddy door open and the shouts of "Cast off!" and "Up anchor!" He even tried to keep his teeth from chattering as the damp December wind swept over him, just in case someone could hear him.

As he'd hoped, the boat eased away from the dock and began to dip and rock and sway its way down the Ashley. When the only sound he could hear was the puffing of the steam, he risked raising his chin to see.

They were just passing a bluff that overlooked the river, from which an ancient moss-draped live oak leaned. It seemed to be watching him. In fact, everything seemed to be watching him. The bulrushes on either side of the river blew in his direction. A branch hanging out farther down the shoreline reached for him. Even the flock of wood ducks that squawked and honked overhead seemed to be screaming right at him, *Why did you do this? You know you weren't supposed to!*

"I had to do it," he whispered to them. "I had to be with Charlotte and Henry-James one more time!"

But Austin still felt uneasy. He crawled to a spot on the deck to catch more of the sun that was trying to burn through the cold clouds over the trees, and he stared down into the water.

It was the color of tea that had been brewed too long, except for its greenish tinge. He'd always liked its color—and the way the cypresses and the magnolias and the tulip trees reflected in it. He loved everything about South Carolina he'd learned so far, and there was still so much to find out and do.

He studied a long log that bobbed near the bank. *Take that, for instance,* he thought. *I haven't had a chance to even try walking a log in the water. Henry-James does it so easily.*

But even as he stared longingly at the fallen tree trunk, it seemed to rise up out of the water.

It *did* rise out of the water. And it brought up a wide, scaly tail and slapped it angrily as it plunged out into the river. Two hooded eyes blinked from the top of a long pointed snout.

Austin forgot to be quiet. "It's an alligator!" he screamed. "It's an alligator!"

He stared, hands frozen to the deck, heart slamming so hard that he could feel it in his ears. There was no telling how long he would have stayed there if a black hand hadn't closed around his arm.

"Massa Austin!" Henry-James hissed. "What you *doin'* here?"

Austin managed to shake himself to life and pointed, trembling, toward the water. "It was an alligator, Henry-James!"

Henry-James clapped his hand over Austin's mouth and dragged him to a corner of the deck. There was a large coil of rope there, and Henry-James picked Austin up under the armpits and dumped him into the center of it. Only his head stuck out, and Henry-James pressed that down with a big hand.

"You keep your silly self outta sight, Massa Austin," he whispered hoarsely, "or you gonna be in a heap o' trouble!"

"Will it get us?" Austin said.

"Will what get us?"

"That alligator."

"What you talkin' 'bout, Massa Austin?" Henry-James said in disgust. "That gator ain't no match for this here boat."

Of course it wasn't. Austin blinked and felt like a ninny. Henry-James was shaking his head at him. "You got a lot worse to worry 'bout than some alligator, once Marse Drayton find out you done stowed away on this boat."

Austin poked his head up above the rope coil. "I don't care," he said. "I was afraid my father would come or send for us while you were gone. I couldn't leave with things like this—not knowing what was going to happen and all."

Henry-James licked his lips. "I declare, Massa Austin, you the most bullheaded chil' I ever knowed."

"You're going to be glad I am, too," Austin said.

"Why?"

"Don't I always think of something when there's trouble?"

Henry-James glanced nervously over his shoulder. "You ain't never knowed the kind o' trouble we talkin' 'bout now, Massa Austin. I don't think I have neither. They's talkin' war and such."

Austin folded his arms along the top of the coil. "Will they make you go and fight in it, do you think?"

Henry-James chewed at his wet lip. "Miz Kady say she think they could—or Marse Drayton could take me 'long as his body slave if'n he went." He looked out over the river, and his mouth moved again, though Austin could barely catch what he said.

It sounded like, "But she say it don't got to come to that."

"What did you say?" Austin said.

But a door creaked open below them, and Henry-James's eyes bulged. He thrust Austin's head down with the palm of his hand and tensed up to listen.

"Henry-James!" Isaac's voice bellowed over the water. "Where you at, boy?"

"Up here!" Henry-James said. "I be right down."

The door creaked shut again, and Austin looked out of the damp coil to see Henry-James glaring down at him.

"What you gonna do when we gets there, Massa Austin?" he said. "I hope you got you a plan, 'cause I ain't gonna be able to give you much help. I gots Marse Drayton to look after."

"I'll think of something," Austin said.

"Well, you do it with your head inside this here rope or you ain't gonna need no plan," Henry-James said sternly. "You gonna need a savior!"

Austin nodded and scrunched down lower in the coil. He felt better now that Henry-James knew he was there. "Will you tell Charlotte?" he whispered.

"If'n I gets the chance," Henry-James said. "Now you stay low. And take this."

He thrust something down into the coiled rope.

"What is it?" Austin said, feeling the cloth.

"My workin' hat," Henry-James said. "I got to change into my fancy uniform 'fore we goes into Charleston. You wear that low over your face so don't nobody recognize you, you hear?"

Austin grinned to himself and pulled Henry-James's floppy felt hat over his eyes. He felt even better wearing it.

It might have been the longest trip to Charleston Austin had ever taken, but their arrival was worth it. Even before the boat pulled alongside the pier, Austin could hear the excitement. People shouted, music drifted down to the pier from the middle of town, and there were twice as many horses' hooves clopping over the cobblestone streets as usual.

Everyone in South Carolina is here for this, Austin thought. *I couldn't miss it.*

It took all the patience he had to stay twisted into a little knot within the ropes while Isaac, Henry-James, and the others got the boat docked and the Ravenals streamed out of the cabin and down the gangplank.

"What time is it?" he heard Kady ask.

"Nearly one," Uncle Drayton said. "We've got to hurry."

"Where are we going, Drayton?" Aunt Olivia said, her shrill voice carrying over the anxious buzz of the crowd. "I want to go to the house and freshen up."

"There's no time for that," Uncle Drayton said. "I want to get to St. Andrew's Hall."

Their voices trailed off, and Austin raised his head cautiously so that only his eyes appeared above the coiled rope. He was just in time to see Henry-James climb up onto the driver's seat of the green carriage and raise the reins. At the same time, he peered toward the boat and gave the tiniest nod.

The moment the carriage pulled away, Austin sprang from his hiding place and, with legs stiff as posts, clambered down the ladder and down the gangplank. Trying to keep the carriage in sight with the hat pulled over his eyes was hard, but he couldn't help grinning to himself.

Wait till I tell Charlotte about this *adventure*, he thought.

Fortunately, the carriage couldn't travel fast, what with the streets clogged with wagons, carriages, and carts of every description. Austin tucked himself into the crowds on the sidewalk and stayed close on the trail of the Ravenals as they made their labored way toward St. Andrew's Hall.

By the time they got to Broad Street, there was no room for vehicles at all. Austin hung back in the throng of people as Uncle Drayton abandoned the carriage and led his family into the street on foot, leaving Henry-James to mind the horses.

Don't worry, Henry-James, Austin thought. *I'll remember every detail to tell you.*

"What's taking them so long in there?" a stranger behind him asked someone else.

"There're 160 delegates," that someone answered. "They can't all agree just like that!"

"Why not?" somebody else chimed in. "We've got no choice but to secede. Everybody knows it."

"Not everybody. You've seen all those books, sayin' slavery was holdin' the South back."

"Yes, and we burned them, didn't we? And their authors, too!"

There was a chorus of harsh laughter. Austin tried to shrink into his jacket. He pulled the rim of his hat still lower over his face, just in case they might consider burning the *son* of one of those authors as well.

There wasn't much time to worry about that, however, for just then the ornate front doors of the Hall of St. Andrew's Society were pushed open, and the sea of heads crowned with bowlers and stovepipe hats craned toward them. The crowd seemed to hold its breath as one.

Austin was too far away to see the face of the person who emerged onto the top of the steps and lifted a paper. He could only strain to listen.

"At one quarter past the hour of one o'clock," the man shouted, "the delegates to the South Carolina state convention voted—unanimously—to dissolve the Union between the State of South Carolina and other states united with her under the compact entitled 'The Constitution of the United States of America.' "

No one heard the rest. There was a roar from the crowd so loud that Austin would have covered his ears to avoid being deafened by it—if he had been able to move.

But he could only stand amid the cheering, almost hysterical mob and think one stunned and frozen thought: *Charlotte and I don't belong to the same country anymore.*

It was like a bad dream just before dawn. It seemed real, and yet it couldn't possibly be. No one around him seemed to be having a hard time believing it. It took a blast from someone's horn to quiet the people again.

"There will be an official signing ceremony at Institute Hall at seven o'clock this evening," the man on the steps of St. Andrew's shouted.

Once again the horde went wild. This time, Austin squeezed among the hoop skirts and greatcoats and caught sight of the Ravenal carriage. Uncle Drayton was just helping the girls and Aunt Olivia inside, and Henry-James was in the driver's seat, scanning the crowd with his eyes. Austin took a chance and waved at him. Henry-James nodded his head and jerked it ever so slightly toward the opposite corner.

There was a wagon parked there, and aboard were Isaac, Mousie, and Tot, waiting patiently for Uncle Drayton's next orders. Wherever the family was going, they were obviously going to go, too. Slipping like a shadow between the hurrying people, Austin headed for the wagon. Just as Isaac clicked his tongue at the horses, Austin's lanky arms and legs groped for the back and he swung himself up and over the gate. He landed in a sprawl at Tot's feet.

"Lawdy mercy!" she cried out.

"Shhh—hush!" Austin whispered. It was ridiculous, of course. The din of the streets was so loud that no one would have heard if he'd shot off a cannon in the back of the wagon.

Beside Tot, Mousie squeaked and began clasping and unclasping her hands. Big-muscled Isaac glanced over his shoulder and grunted.

"Henry-James tol' me you'd be comin' along," he said. He shook his head. "I wouldn't want to be in your shoes if'n Marse Drayton catch you. No sirree!"

"Don't worry," Austin said. "Even if he does, I'll tell him you didn't have anything to do with it."

Isaac grunted again and turned back around to drive the

wagon on to the East Battery, where Uncle Drayton's townhouse was. Tot, on the other hand, couldn't seem to take her eyes off Austin. She stared, open-mouthed and saucer-eyed.

"Do you have a blanket or something I can hide under?" Austin said.

She stared. Mousie sighed and produced one. Austin was sure poor Tot was still gaping when he wriggled under the blanket and out of sight.

When the wagon rocked to a stop in the carriage house, Austin tried to turn himself into a statute, although everything on his body chose that moment to start itching, and the coarse wool blanket didn't help. He was willing himself not to scratch as Tot, Mousie, and Isaac unloaded the wagon. Just then he heard Henry-James hiss to him.

"I'm here," Austin whispered.

"And you gots to stay there, Massa Austin," Henry-James said. "Marse Drayton, he in the blackest mood I ever seen him in. He even yell at Missus to keep her mouth shut."

"What's happening?"

"That's just it. He don't know. Now that them committee people done decided to break away, he don't know what's to become of him. We gon' stay for that there ceremony while he think what to do."

"I'm missing everything," Austin said, giving in and going after the itch on his neck with his fingernails.

"You lucky," Henry-James said. "I could hear Miz Polly wailing 'bout them parties she gonna miss all the way up on the driver's seat!"

"Does Charlotte know I'm here yet?"

"I ain't had a chance to tell her. You just stay put there, Massa Austin. I take care o' that."

It would have been a long five hours if he hadn't. As it was, Austin thought he'd go mad curled up under the blanket, his toes going numb and the wool scratching his face. But after what seemed like two days at least, he felt the wagon rock, and he heard Charlotte whisper, "Are you in there, Boston?"

"I'm here," Austin said. "Is anybody looking? I have to get out from under this thing before I suffocate!"

She giggled and pulled the blanket off him. She had to put her hands over her mouth to keep from laughing out loud.

"What's so funny?" Austin whispered.

"You," she said. "I'd take you for a beggar any day!"

"Good," Austin whispered. "At least that way nobody will recognize me."

"Why are you whispering? Everyone is inside arguing. They can't hear us out here."

"Are they eating?" Austin said. "I'm starving."

Charlotte grinned and unwrapped a napkin she'd placed on the floor of the wagon. Two peppermint cakes gleamed up at him.

He polished both of them off before Charlotte said, "I'm glad you came, Boston. Everyone else is so grumpy."

"Because of the secession?"

She nodded. "Daddy says he thinks that he's either going to have to join them or we'll have to move to the North. He's waiting to see what the 'mood of the crowd' is after the ceremony."

"Move?" Austin said. "You mean, leave Canaan Grove?"

Charlotte shook her head. "That just isn't going to happen, you know. He's just upset."

"I don't know," Austin said. "People have started throwing rocks through windows and all of that. Once it's official, things could get worse."

"Austin—"

"But leave the plantation? That would be awful. What about all the slaves?"

"Austin—"

"What about Henry-James and Ria and Daddy Elias? How

could you live without the swamps and the gardens and all? We don't have those up north—"

"Austin!"

Austin stopped. Charlotte was ghostly white, and she had her hands on the sides of her face as if she were holding it in place.

"You aren't making me feel better," she said. "You're making it worse."

She was right. He was starting to feel that fear in his chest again, and it was causing a lump in his throat that could easily turn into tears if he wasn't careful. This wasn't the time for wallowing around in how bad things were. This was a time for making the situation better. It wasn't going to be easy—

"It ain't always easy," Daddy Elias had told him. *"You got to find that there narrow gate."*

Narrow gate. Was this it?

It didn't matter. What mattered now was what Charlotte was expecting him to do—make it better.

"All right, then," Austin said. "We've stood up to those Fire Eaters before. We've even outsmarted the Patty Rollers and those mean boys in Flat Rock. There's plenty we can do about this."

Charlotte's eyes lit up hopefully. "Like what?"

Austin wasn't sure. He said the first thing that came into his mind. "We can refuse to change everything just because these people want to," he said. "We'll talk Uncle Drayton into still having Christmas when we get back to Canaan Grove, and maybe even into coming here for the season." He started to warm to the subject. "Even if my father does send for us, I still have plenty of time. We could take turns being lookouts at night, you, me, Polly, Kady, and Henry-James. Maybe Tot would even take a shift—no, she's too scatterbrained. But Bogie could help. We could keep vigils to watch for attacking Fire Eaters, and we might even be able to give them a taste of their own medicine, you know? Be ready with rocks to throw back, not to hit them with, mind you, just to give them a scare, let them know we're not to be toyed with—"

He stopped. Charlotte was covering her mouth and laughing.

"Now what's so funny?" he said.

"You haven't even taken a breath!" she said.

"We haven't got time to breathe," Austin said. "We've got work to do!"

"What are you going to do lying here under this blanket?" she said.

"Think. Plan. Pray, too. I'm sure Jesus has some good ideas." He gave her a nudge. "You go find out everything you can about Uncle Drayton's plans. And start dropping hints about Christmas and the season. Get Polly and Kady to help you."

"Polly won't help."

"Yes, she will. She says she'll die if she doesn't get to put on a fancy gown and flirt with all the boys!"

"Oh, that's right."

Austin nodded firmly at her. "You have to get started, Lottie," he said. "We can't let them lick us."

It was a thought worth itching under a blanket all afternoon for.

By the time the wagon headed back to Meeting Street—and Mousie smuggled him a piece of cornbread slathered in strawberry preserves—it was dark, and he felt safe sitting up and peeking over the side of the wagon. Charleston was an unbelievable sight.

Charlestonians thronged the street, their hats and lapels covered in cockades of South Carolina palmetto fronds and blue ribbons. Church bells chimed out of control. Carolina flags were frantically waved. Shops were decked out with bunting. Every other person seemed to be carrying a placard that said The Union Is Dissolved! Every few minutes a cannon was fired, sending Mousie and Tot retreating under Austin's abandoned blanket.

It was impossible to get the carriage and the wagon past

Chalmers Street. Austin heard Uncle Drayton shout to Henry-James and Isaac to stop and let them all out to walk the rest of the way.

There was no end to the complaints from Aunt Olivia. Even from a distance, Austin could see her chins quivering at triple-time, and he was happy to hang back so he didn't have to hear her. He just kept his eyes on Uncle Drayton's stovepipe hat and followed, although he did take a moment to stare through the blaze of torches and gaslights at the South Carolina Institute Hall.

It was like a palace, right out of the Renaissance as far as Austin could tell from having read about it in books. It was a glorious place, with dozens of arched windows and columns and fancy plasterwork.

Too bad they're using it to do something so stupid, Austin thought.

He was getting used to being the only one who felt that way. All around him, voices were raised in jubilation. There were so many that Austin could only pick out a few at a time.

"It's time we did this! It's time we built a southern republic out of the ruins of the Union!"

"It's a new empire!"

"Overthrow the Union!"

"A confederacy of slave-holding states will take its place!"

One man, who was dressed all in black like a preacher, raised his eyes to the flashing sky, closed his eyes, and cried, "God in heaven, tear down the Yankees! Build up the South!"

Austin shrank back from him, and from the others, until there was no place else to go. This was supposed to be a celebration, but all Austin could see and hear was hatred. He was sure if he reached out, he'd be able to touch it.

And he certainly didn't want to.

For two hours they stood there outside Institute Hall while

the shouting and the cannon fire went on. Austin spent his time keeping Charlotte and Henry-James in sight and trying to shut out the ugly words that came at him like pellets of hail.

"Let the northerners have their reform, their women's suffrage, their education. Let us be independent and keep our slavery!"

"We'll never convince them that slavery for the South is God's will anyway!"

"We saved the Negroes from Africa and converted them to Christianity. What more do they want?"

"The slaves know in their hearts they'd have miserable lives in Africa!"

"What hearts? Slaves don't have hearts—they have gizzards!"

Austin plastered both hands over his ears and squeezed his eyes shut. But he could still feel the evil clawing at him. He thought he would climb out of his skin.

Suddenly, the crowd seemed to come to attention around him. He opened his eyes and saw the same man he'd seen this afternoon emerge from Institute Hall.

"That's Jamison!" someone cried out. "He's president of the convention!"

There was a tense hush, as if thousands of hearts had stopped beating all at once.

Thousands of gizzards, Austin thought angrily. He wanted more than anything to be next to Henry-James right now—to tell him he was a person, not some barnyard fowl.

President Jamison held up a piece of paper and waved it over his head. "I proclaim the State of South Carolina an independent commonwealth!" he cried.

If Austin had thought the town had lost its mind before, he hadn't seen anything yet. Once again, all of Charleston erupted. A military company paraded down the street, parting the mob like Moses parted the Red Sea. From the Battery, he heard a salute being fired. A bonfire, made of a barrel of rosin, burst out on the street corner. Before he could even move, a rocket glared across the sky, and two boys down by the Circular Congregational Church set off firecrackers.

It was a wild frenzy of celebration, and it made Austin's chest burn. All he wanted to do was find Henry-James and Charlotte—and he didn't care if Uncle Drayton saw him or not. This was frightening, and he didn't want to be in it alone.

Standing on his tiptoes, Austin pushed his hat back from his face and stretched his neck to look for the Ravenals or Isaac or someone he knew. A man waving a torch jostled roughly past him, knocking the floppy felt hat right off Austin's head. Frantically, he reached down to grab it. When he came back up, the man with the torch was searching his face with his eyes.

Austin choked back a gasp. It was Virgil Rhett.

"Hey, now," Rhett said. His eyebrows drew into a tangle. "You're Ravenal's nephew."

Austin turned with a jerk to run, but Rhett curled his fingers around Austin's arm. His face was as fiery as his torch.

"You're that abolitionist's son!" he cried.

"Who's an abolitionist?" someone else shouted.

Heads turned. Eyes glared. And Austin was suddenly in the center of a circle of hate.

"This boy?" someone cried.

"Yes!"

"Then get him!" they shouted. "Grab him!"

✝ ✝ ✝

Chapter Five

ands suddenly seemed to come from everywhere. People must have had three or four apiece, Austin was sure. Faces contorted in hate, they all lunged to grab him.

Austin didn't freeze this time. With his heart thundering in his chest, he wrenched himself away from Virgil Rhett, ducked the flying arms, and tried to dive between two men in wool frock coats. Someone behind him grabbed at his ankle and he stumbled, becoming hopelessly entangled in a man's coattails. For a moment, there was confusion.

"Where is he?"

"He's caught here! I've got him!"

"Grab the brat!"

"Don't let him get away!"

It was in that moment that Austin unraveled himself and wedged his way into the midst of a crowd of ladies in secession bonnets. For the first time in his life, he was thankful for hoop skirts that seemed to stretch for miles.

The outraged shouting of Virgil and his group was soon smothered in the cannon fire and band music. But Austin didn't stop running and weaving and dodging. Down Chalmers Street he went, not even taking time to shiver at the sight of the slave market. Even the alley at the end didn't scare him. In fact, it invited him in, and he tore down it, slipping on garbage and leaping over a startled rat or two until he emerged on another street and flailed wildly amid the crowd.

"Watch it now, boy!" someone scolded him.

"What's he running from?" Austin heard someone ask.

It was time to get out of sight. With a sinking heart, he realized he'd been running in the opposite direction from the wagon, and he wasn't at all sure where he was.

I haven't had time to explore Charleston, he thought. *I don't know where anything is.*

Confusion wasn't something Austin Hutchinson felt very often. He had to get to a place where he could stop running and figure this out.

Just ahead, another narrow alley beckoned him. Flattening himself between the wall and a merchant's cart piled with cockaded bonnets, Austin made for the alley. At the corner, his foot skidded on the slippery brick sidewalk and flew crazily to one side. The cart rocked, and a stack of bonnets teetered and spilled over into the street.

"Hey, now! Who did that?" the merchant cried.

Austin took off into the alley with his heels flying up behind him. At the sight of a door in the back of the building that abutted the alley, he felt hope. To his relief it came open when he pulled on it, and he closed himself inside and leaned against it, breathing like Uncle Drayton's steam packet.

As he caught his breath, he looked around. It was dark, and for a moment he couldn't see anything. Finally, shapes began to emerge out of the blackness: a broom, a mop, several buckets, and a wash tub. There was an outline of light across from him that had to be another door. Austin went toward it, but he stopped with his hand on the knob. There were voices coming from the other side.

"Let's go out and join the celebration," he heard a man's voice say. "Heaven knows we've earned it!"

"Let them have their party," another man said. "If we don't keep at this, there won't be anything to celebrate."

"Whatever do you mean? We've declared our independence!"

"And now we're going to have to fight for it, make no mistake about that."

"All right," said someone else. "What's our next step?"

The serious voice grumbled for a second. Austin pressed his ear against the door.

"Since we're our own nation now," the man said finally, "based on the principle of slavery, anyone who declares himself an abolitionist is a traitor."

"Indeed!"

"So any one of them who sets foot in the commonwealth of South Carolina will have to be arrested."

Austin's chest felt as if it were being seized by angry fingers. He hoped the men inside couldn't hear his heart pounding.

I must be in the back of Institute Hall, he thought. *I've stepped right into the hands of those Fire Eaters!*

"Names," said one of the men. "Give us a list of names so we can get the word out."

The serious man began to rattle off a list. Austin edged toward the door he'd come through from the alley.

"Gerrit Smith, Anthony Burns, John Rankin . . ."

Austin held his breath and felt for the doorknob.

"Levi Coffin," the man continued. "Wesley Hutchinson."

Austin fell against the door with a thud.

"What was that?" said someone inside.

"It came from the storeroom. Go see."

Heart throbbing in his throat, Austin yanked open the door and hurled himself out into the alley. Behind him, brooms and mops clattered to the floor, and a voice called out, "Who's that? You there—stop!"

Austin, of course, didn't stop. Instead, he pumped his arms and his legs like train pistons as he raced down the alley. Footsteps pounded out onto the bricks behind him and drew closer, no matter how furiously Austin drove his legs and arms.

Please, Lord, he prayed in his head. *Please don't let them catch me!*

God's answer was a crowd milling at the end of the alley. Austin dove into it almost headfirst and scrambled through the swaying skirts of a group of ladies who were so busy shouting the praises of the South they didn't even notice him. He darted and wove through the crowd until his side ached and he couldn't run anymore. He pressed himself against a wall and searched for anyone still coming after him. There was no one, but his heart wouldn't slow down.

I bet the Ravenals have left me! he thought. *I'm going to have to run all the way back to the townhouse.*

But where is *the house?*

Austin twisted around and tried to find something familiar. But nothing looked the same as it had previously, not with a bonfire in a barrel on every corner, placards covering every wall, and the sky crisscrossed with rockets. He didn't see anything he'd ever seen before . . . except the wagon at the end of the street. The wagon with Isaac at the reins and two scarved heads poking up from the back. Even as he recognized it, it moved forward with a jerk.

"No!" Austin cried. "Wait! Wait for me!"

But the horses tossed their heads and disappeared behind the corner building. Gasping for the last of his air, Austin hurled himself toward it. He knocked over a barrel, tripped over the corner of a lady's cape, and nearly sprawled into another cart where a man was selling cockades and hot apple cider. But he kept running—and the wagon kept going, making its way up Meeting Street in fits and starts, away from the direction of the townhouse.

"Wait!" Austin cried again. But it didn't. Austin had to run in its wake, nearly colliding with a horse pulling a shay. With the steed breathing down his neck, he threw his hands up and grabbed the back of the wagon. Only then did Tot and Mousie see him.

"Lawdy, it's Massa Austin!" Tot cried.

It took Isaac only a split second to slow the wagon and yell, "Pull him in! Pull him in!"

With much clutching and yanking, the two slave women were able to haul Austin over the back of the wagon. He lay on its floor, not knowing whether to laugh or burst out crying.

"Massa Austin?" Mousie said in her timid voice. "You want some cornbread?"

Austin chose laughing. He threw his head back to howl, and as he did, he caught a glimpse of something hurtling through the air.

"Marse Drayton!" Isaac cried. "Look out!"

The green Ravenal carriage was just ahead of them. The object in the air hit it soundly on the side and splattered. After it came another, and then another, until the air seemed filled with flying fruit and vegetables.

"You're a traitor, Ravenal!" voices shouted. "Join us—or leave South Carolina!"

Austin wanted to scream back at them. But all he could do was throw the blanket over his head and hide.

Only because everyone was so upset by the attack from the crowd was Austin able to hide in the cuddy with Isaac and Henry-James all the way up the river and get up to his mother's room at Canaan Grove without anyone seeing him.

She was wide awake and waiting for him.

"You went with them, didn't you?" she said. Her eyes were big in her frightened face.

Austin felt horrible as he sank down on the bed next to her. Scaring her hadn't been what he'd meant to do at all. He'd made another mess.

"I didn't plan to," he said. "Honest. It just happened. I

couldn't imagine not ever seeing them again—"

"Why would that be?" she said.

"If Father came to get us while they were gone—"

Sally Hutchinson was shaking her head. "I would never do that to you, Austin. I know these are difficult times, but some things just have to be done, no matter what we have to endure to get them done. Saying good-bye is one of those things."

Austin nodded, but he didn't feel much better. She always knew the right thing to say and do. He just didn't—no matter how hard he tried.

She was watching him closely. "Did any good come of your trip?" she said.

"Good?" he said.

She folded her arms around her knees. "Should I be glad you went?"

He thought for a second. "Maybe," he said. "I did hear something."

He poured out all that had happened in Charleston. As he talked, her already pale face turned the pasty color of grits.

"Austin," she said, "this is even worse than I thought. They actually mentioned your father's name?"

Austin nodded. "They'll arrest him if he tries to come here."

"Then he simply can't come for us, that's all there is to it." She tossed back the covers and threw her feet over the side of the bed. "Fetch me my pen and ink, will you?" she said. "I have to get word to him at once."

"Isn't there any other way?" Austin said.

She shook her head sadly. "I don't think so. When you have your own children, you'll understand. Their safety comes first."

Austin dragged himself to the secretary and took out the pen, ink, and paper. He sat down and dipped the pen tip into the well.

"What do you want me to write?" he said.

"Well, 'Dear Wesley,' of course."

He wrote that. Then he stopped.

"What is it?" she said.

"I try to do what's right, you know? I pray and I talk to Daddy Elias and I try. But sometimes, I don't know what's right to do."

"What don't you know?"

"It doesn't feel like it's time to go yet. There are things . . ."

"What things?" she said.

He shrugged. His mother touched his cheek, just enough so he wouldn't get embarrassed, before she pulled her hand away.

"My clever Austin," she said. "Sometimes it gets so deep in that mind of yours that even I don't know what to say to you. But think of it this way—whatever 'things' you have to do before you go, this delay gives you a little bit of time, doesn't it?"

Austin gave that some thought.

Then he wrote the letter in his best penmanship and grammar. "Don't try to come openly into South Carolina," they told Father. "The Fire Eaters are after you."

Austin sighed as he watched his mother seal the letter with wax. She was right—at least this meant he and Charlotte could move on with their plan. That made him feel a little less heavy. All those hours of planning hadn't been wasted.

The very next morning, while Uncle Drayton sat miserably over his stewed peaches and bread and clabber, and Aunt Olivia fussed nervously with her tea, Austin said to the breakfast gathering, "I don't think it's fair for those people to take away our Christmas."

Aunt Olivia waved him off with a jeweled hand. Beside him, Polly sniffed loudly, and behind *her*, Tot fumbled for the hand-kerchief she could never find.

But across the table, Kady sat up straight in her chair.

"Really, Austin?" she said. "You think we should still celebrate Christmas?"

"I've never had a Christmas, not that I can remember," he said. "We're always traveling."

Kady's honey-brown eyes sprang open. "Never? Really?"

Austin shook his head. It was the truth, and it was turning out to be a handy little piece of truth at that.

"Mama," Kady said, "I don't see how we can *not* have our usual celebration. That would be criminal!"

"Then call me a thief," Aunt Olivia said, tossing her pile of elaborate curls and, of course, setting her chins to wiggling as a result. "I am in no mood—"

"Then perhaps we should get in one."

They all turned to stare at Uncle Drayton, then Austin exchanged glances with Charlotte. She was as wide-eyed as he knew he was.

"Austin is right," Uncle Drayton said. "There is no reason whatsoever why this whole political mess should destroy our family traditions." He was trying to make his voice sound cheerful, but Austin detected the sadness in his eyes. "This may be the last Christmas we will be able to celebrate here—or with Sally and the boys."

Aunt Olivia didn't look as if that last point bothered her too much, but she did stop dabbing at her eyes long enough to consider the idea.

"We've only a few days to prepare," she said.

"But we already started before we went to Charleston!" Polly said. Her limp, sausage-like curls were quivering. "The garlands are nearly done, and we have enough candles now."

"Come on, then, Mama," Kady said. "If we all turn to—"

"It will do you good, Livvy," Uncle Drayton said. "And what other use will you have for that new dress you had made for the holidays?"

That did it. No one even finished breakfast as the dishes were swept away and the candles and garlands produced. Within hours there were festoons of boxwood and crabapple decorating every side of the house outside and candles lighting every window.

Once that was done, there wasn't a spot on the plantation that wasn't bustling with the rest of the preparations, and Austin and Charlotte were right in the thick of them.

The kitchen building oozed the smells of plum pudding and gingerbread that Austin and Charlotte and even Jefferson were allowed to help Josephine roll out. They followed her to the smokehouse where she picked out just the right hams cured with green hickory wood and the perfect side of beef hanging over its oak log. Austin and Henry-James chased down a big turkey, though Austin couldn't stand by and watch it meet the hatchet.

The sewing slaves were everywhere, knitting and stitching and creating piles of mysterious things. Austin didn't find out what those were until a line of knitted stockings appeared hanging on the stairs.

"What are those for?" he asked Charlotte.

"Haven't you ever heard the poem—you know, 'A Visit From St. Nicholas'?"

Austin shook his head.

" 'The stockings were hung by the chimney with care'?" she quoted.

"I don't know that one," Austin said. "Is it by Keats? Shelley?"

Charlotte patted his arm. "You really *have* missed Christmas, haven't you? What do you want for your present?"

"Present?" he said. "You mean a gift?"

"Of course," she said. "We always give each other presents on Christmas."

"I don't have one for you!" Austin said.

"I always make mine," she said. "You'll think of something."

There wasn't much time to think, not with all there was to do. On December 22, Charlotte, Austin, and Jefferson followed Aunt Olivia down to Slave Street and helped her give sugar candy to all the children. Henry-James was no longer considered a child, but Charlotte slipped him some anyway.

On the 23rd, the slaves were given time to do their Christmas preparations. Austin was all over the plantation, watching as his black friends gathered nuts and apples and even eggs. No one would tell him why they needed eggs, no matter how many times he asked. The women, even Ria, busily sewed scraps of lace and beads they'd found onto their clothes, and most of them made gingerbread. Austin watched in fascination as Ria put her dough into a round oven with legs on it and no handle and pulled out a loaf of bread that looked and smelled every bit as good as what they'd made up in the kitchen building.

That night the children were invited to Ria and Daddy Elias and Henry-James's cabin to sit by their fire and pop corn and parch peanuts. Ria wouldn't allow Daddy Elias to have any popcorn until he drank all his rosemary tea. Seeing that gave Austin a pang of guilt. He had never talked to his mother about how sick Daddy Elias was. But it gave him an idea.

"I know what my Christmas present is going to be for you, Daddy Elias," he said.

"That's good," he said, "'cause I know I's gonna be faster than you at I-Ketch-Yu."

"What's that?" Austin said.

"You'll see," Henry-James said as he stuffed his mouth with popcorn.

"That's not fair, Henry-James!" Charlotte said. "How can he play the game if he doesn't know the rules?"

"Game?" Jefferson said. He spewed popcorn across the hearth.

"What are the rules?" Austin said.

"I better tell it or we'll be here all night," said the always serious Ria. "If a slave says 'Merry Christmas' or 'Christmas gift' to you before you can say it to him, you gots to give him a gift."

"And then we gives you one," Henry-James said.

Charlotte giggled. "You'll really like this game, Austin."

"I like it already!" Jefferson said. "I like presents!"

"That sounds like a lot of presents," Austin said. He went to work right then, thinking up what to give.

The next day, Christmas Eve, was the busiest yet. That was the day Aunt Olivia and Uncle Drayton—helped by Kady and Polly, who dressed up like a plantation mistress for the occasion and was most gracious to the slaves—gave extra rations to their workers.

Austin felt like *he* was getting the presents, the way his heart swelled up every time a black face beamed when presented with a package of meat, salt, rice, and molasses. There was even some coffee given out and bags of sweet potatoes and a blanket for each cabin.

"I like Christmas," Austin said to Charlotte.

She grinned. "You haven't seen anything yet, Boston."

And she was right. Before Austin even had his eyes open on Christmas morning, he heard music from below—violins and drums. Jefferson was already sitting up in bed, rubbing his eyes and jabbering about the presents.

Austin ran to the window and looked down. The back porch was crowded with slave musicians and dancers, all in green and white with their bits of lace and beads sparkling in the early morning sun. On the steps were five little girls, hands folded as if they were waiting.

"Come on!" Charlotte said from their bedroom doorway. "Don't miss the carolers!"

They tore downstairs, still in their nightshifts—though they had to drag Jefferson past the bulging stockings. The early morning frosty air bit at their noses as they stood among the musicians and listened to the little girls sing like angels.

Brightly does the morning break
In the eastern sky; awake!
Cradled on his bed of hay
Jesus Christ was born today.
Let a merry Christmas be,

Massa, both to me and thee!

"And it shall be," Uncle Drayton cried from the porch.

"Merry Christmas!" the children all shouted. "Christmas gifts!"

Uncle Drayton threw back his head and laughed in the trumpeting way that Austin hadn't heard for weeks. His uncle grabbed a large bag and made his way down the steps while the children clamored around him. Austin noticed they were all holding napkins full of something he couldn't identify.

"Merry Christmas!" each child said again. And each time, Uncle Drayton produced a gift. Mostly it looked like knitted caps with tabs that went over the ears and strings that tied under their chins, but they seemed delighted with them. Jefferson, on the other hand, looked a little concerned.

With every gift Uncle Drayton handed out, Aunt Olivia received a napkin bundle from a slave.

"What's in those?" Austin asked.

Charlotte giggled. "Eggs!" she said.

Austin tried not to look disappointed. "Oh," he said. "I guess eggs are nice."

"I don't want eggs!" Charlotte said. "They give us apples and nuts and things, but I always end up giving them back somehow because they don't have that much."

"Sing and dance and make merry!" Uncle Drayton cried out to the slaves. "Dinner will be served at noon!"

The slaves all cheered and commenced to kicking up their heels, many of them barefoot on the icy-cold porch. Uncle Drayton ushered the family inside, where they gathered in the drawing room.

The gifts he handed out were much different. Jefferson was presented with a miniature firefighter, a toy train called a carpet runner that moved on the floor, and a stack of picture books with birds that flew and musicians that strummed their banjos when he pulled ribbons. For Austin there was a game called Geographical Lotto, which he couldn't wait to get into, and a box filled with leather-bound books that smelled like Uncle Drayton's library.

"Those are some I picked out for you," Uncle Drayton said. "I want you to have them."

Austin felt a little swell of pride. It was sad, too—but there was no time for that, not with the squeals from Polly and Aunt Olivia over the gowns Uncle Drayton had made for them, all with matching fans, shoes, and hair fixings. Charlotte wasn't as happy with her china doll dressed in silk to match the dress for herself that Aunt Olivia said might finally make her want to be a lady. But Charlotte's eyes lit up like the tallow candle flames when Uncle Drayton presented the gift he said was for all the children.

It was a huge thing, so large they all had to go out in the hall. It was made up of a long board of yellow pine that dipped in the middle and was attached at either end onto two upside down T's joined in the middle.

"It's a joggling board!" Charlotte cried.

Before Austin could ask what you did with such a thing, Charlotte leaped onto it. It bounced in the middle, and she shrieked with laughter.

"I haven't seen one of those in years!" Mother said. "Do you remember the one we had, Drayton?"

Uncle Drayton smiled wistfully. "We spent hours on that— rocking and talking."

"And you trying to bounce me off!" she said.

"I never did anything of the kind. Your mother lies, Austin!"

But Austin had long since stopped listening to them. He was on the joggling board, rocking and howling with Charlotte. Jefferson joined them, then Kady, and finally even Polly.

"Well, one thing is for sure," Aunt Olivia announced over the squealing. "There was never an unmarried daughter at the home that had a joggling board."

Polly beamed at that. Kady shot her mother a sharp look.

"Why is that?" Austin said. "I don't get it."

"It's just a silly legend," Kady said.

"No, it isn't," Aunt Olivia said. "It's the perfect spot for courting. Why, Drayton and I—"

"Let's spare them the details," Uncle Drayton said.

Everyone laughed—except Kady. Austin watched her face darken as if a shadow had just passed through her mind.

Aunt Olivia still wants her to marry some Charleston boy, he thought. *And she still doesn't want to.*

But the shadow passed, and the music went on, and so did the dancing and laughing and eating.

Austin had been to Ravenal family celebrations before and thought that those had provided more food than he had ever seen in one place. But this day outdid them all.

Even for the slaves, there were plum puddings and gingerbread, apples and oranges, and plates of ham, goose, and turkey. Pies disappeared in delightful mouthfuls, as did sweet potatoes and thick slices of bread smothered in currant preserves.

The gift-giving went on all day, too. Charlotte gave Austin a book she'd made out of cloth and scraps of parchment. When Austin opened it, it was blank. So was his face.

"You have to write it, Boston," she said. "If you have to go back north, you can write about all our adventures."

Her voice sounded thick. He didn't look at her so she could have a chance to blink back the tears.

"This is my favorite present I've gotten," he whispered to her. "Mine for you isn't as good—I mean, it isn't something you can hold. I didn't have time to—"

"What is it?" Charlotte said. "You do go on sometimes!"

Austin shrugged and poked his toe at the carpet. "I'm just giving you a promise that I'll write to you every week when—if—we have to leave."

He still didn't look at her—even when she threw her arms around his neck and then let go and ran. He decided that meant she liked it.

It was dark before he had a chance to get out to the slave cabin to give his present to Daddy Elias. He had it all worked out with his mother and Uncle Drayton, and he was more excited about giving this gift than any other.

"Merry Christmas!" he called in at the door.

Daddy Elias was in his chair by the fire, smiling through the flicker of firelight that played across his face. The glow made him look younger—and made Austin feel like maybe he wasn't so sick and old after all. It was a happy thought.

"I have the best gift for you," Austin said. "The *best*."

Daddy Elias just smiled.

"Uncle Drayton and Mother both said you should have Ria to take care of you every day until you get well. Right here in your cabin. She doesn't have to go do any other work unless Mother gets really sick, which she won't because she's practically cured."

Austin took a breath, and he saw the shimmer in Daddy Elias's eyes. He looked very young then. Most people do, Austin decided, when they cry.

The old man reached out to touch his hand, but the door flew open and with it came a blast of cold air and Henry-James and Bogie. Bogie whimpered nervously and came over to lick Austin's hand.

"Massa Austin," Henry-James said. "You got to come quick. A message just come."

"From who?" Austin said.

Henry-James gnawed at his lower lip. "From your daddy, Massa Austin. From Wesley Hutchinson hisself."

✠ ✠ ✠

Chapter Six

ustin could hardly get his legs to move as he made his way back to the Big House. He almost expected to see every candle extinguished and the garlands gone, but there were still sparkles in every window, and most of the slaves continued to dance in the cold on the back porch.

It can't be anything much, then, Austin thought hopefully. *Surely it can't be Father sending for us already. Of course not. He couldn't even have received our letter yet.*

But when he got to the drawing room, where everyone was gathered, he knew it *was* something. Something very serious. Faces were stiff and stunned and white. All except Aunt Olivia's. She looked for all the world as if she were holding back a smile.

Austin went right to his mother's side, and he looked for Charlotte. She was sitting close to Kady, looking quivery.

Mother ran a hand over his head. "We've heard from your father," she said. "As soon as he got word of the secession, he arranged for us to go north."

"I still don't think this is safe, Aunt Sally," Kady said.

Uncle Drayton frowned at her. "Now, Kadydid, what could you possibly know about all this? Wesley has arranged for them to go to Major Robert Anderson at Fort Johnson on James Island. It's a Union fort. They'll be safe there."

"You know the secessionists already think all those forts belong to the South now," Kady said. "Not the United States. Fort Sumter, all of them—"

"And that's exactly why Wesley wants us to move quickly," Austin's mother said. "Before the southerners can do anything rash."

"They *will* do something rash, and they'll do it right away," Kady said.

Uncle Drayton's frown narrowed to a steady stare. "When did you become an expert on political affairs?" he said.

"I'm not an expert. I just listened while I was in Charleston. This is affecting our lives. I want to know what's happening."

"Well," Aunt Olivia said, "at least we know one thing. Sally and the boys are leaving. That's settled."

It seemed that it was. Just like that. Across the room from him, Charlotte stared at him for a long minute until her eyes looked like they'd overflow. Then she got up and ran out, setting the wreath on the drawing room door swinging. Austin started to go after her, but his mother caught his wrist.

"Let her go, Austin," she said. "Let's get our things ready and then you can talk to her when she's had a chance to calm down."

There weren't actually many things they could get ready. Father had said in his message to bring only the most necessary belongings for the trip. Uncle Drayton promised he would send the rest later, when they knew where they were going to be.

Here we go, back to living in hotels and train cars again, Austin thought miserably.

By the time his leather satchel was packed with extra stockings and underwear, along with his blank book from Charlotte and the photograph of his father, the lump in his throat was so big that he could hardly talk—and that was saying something for Austin Hutchinson.

But he wanted to talk, and he knew just who he wanted to talk *to*.

He found Daddy Elias the next morning, just getting to his chair from his bed. Ria was there fixing his tea, and Henry-James was on his way out to report to Uncle Drayton.

"I thought the slaves had the two days after Christmas off," Austin said.

"Not the house servants," Henry-James said. "Marse and Missus gots to be tended to no matter what."

"That isn't fair. Do you get gingerbread today, like all the other slave children?"

"I ain't worried none 'bout that," Henry-James said. "I got other things on my mind."

Austin's interest sizzled, and then it died. What was the point in asking? He was leaving anyway.

The lump got even bigger. When Henry-James was gone and Daddy Elias was looking expectantly at Austin, it was a few minutes before he could say anything. Daddy Elias just rocked. Ria just stirred the tea. Bogie just sighed and put his big head in Austin's lap.

And then Austin did start to cry.

"I don't want to leave here!" he burst out.

"I knows, Massa Austin," Daddy Elias said.

"It isn't fair! I'm happy here. I have friends and a home. I don't want to go back up there!"

"I knows, Massa Austin," Daddy Elias said.

"And you know what I hate?"

Daddy Elias shook his head.

"I hate that I can't *do* anything about it! I have to do what my father says, because he's my father, and because he doesn't think it's safe to stay here."

"I knows."

"And the worst part is—" Austin stopped to try to swallow.

"The worst part is, if I just had a little more time . . . What if Charlotte and Henry-James need me? What if *you* need me? Nobody needs me in the North. I just need some more time!"

The crying was threatening to take over, and he had to hold hard to keep it back. Daddy Elias nodded sadly. Ria put a cup of tea in his hand.

"That there has got sugar in it, Massa Austin," she said. "You drink that now."

It was a bigger surprise than any of his Christmas gifts, Ria being kind to him. Austin nodded and, with his eyes and nose streaming, drank the tea. It calmed him down enough to hear what Daddy Elias was saying.

"You know that there narrow gate we was talkin' 'bout just the other day?" the old man said, his spoon mouth soft.

Austin could only nod.

"I think you's about to go through there now. And you know what, Massa Austin?"

"No," Austin said.

"I knows Marse Jesus, and He gonna help you right on through there if you prays. You just see if'n He don't."

Austin didn't know what the old man was talking about. And just then, he was too heartbroken to care. He was drinking his tea in silence when there was a tap at the door. Ria opened it to let Kady in.

"This is a nice surprise, Miz Kady," Ria said. Her face got soft, something that didn't happen very often.

Kady smiled and handed her a pan covered with a towel. "Merry Christmas, Ria," she said. "I know the day-after-Christmas gingerbread is only supposed to be for the children, but I told Mama I didn't care—I was bringing you some." She lowered her voice. "I don't think it's as good as yours, but it's the thought, isn't it?"

Ria nodded happily and so did Daddy Elias. Austin thought

his heart would split wide open. He didn't think he'd ever feel happy again.

"Shouldn't you be getting ready, Austin?" Kady said. "We're leaving in an hour."

Austin's chin came up. "We?"

"Yes, *we*. Hasn't anyone told you? I'm going into Charleston with you."

"Why?" Austin said.

"Daddy has hired a boat pilot and a boat to take you. He thought if anyone recognized our packet there might be attacks on you. But I told him I just didn't think it was right for you and Aunt Sally and Jefferson to go without someone from the family. I'm just going as far as the pier—I'm not even supposed to get off the boat in Charleston."

Austin felt a part of his broken heart knit back together. It wasn't much, but it was something. Just a little more time with Kady.

But that didn't lighten his spirits much when he stood by the river and looked at the faces of his friends—Charlotte, Henry-James, Bogie, and even Polly. Their eyes were so full of everything he was going to miss that it hurt to even look back. He was glad when his mother took him by the hand and led him gently aboard the hired boat. He forced himself not to even glance over his shoulder.

They were all silent behind him. But just as the cabin door closed, he heard a howl.

"That was Bogie," Jefferson said solemnly.

"I know," Austin snapped at him.

He flung himself into a seat and crossed his arms over his chest to try to keep his own tears back. In a few seconds, there was a rustle of linen, and Kady sat down beside him.

"I'm sorry, Austin," Kady said.

"I didn't even have a chance to say good-bye," he said thickly.

"I'll say it for you," she said. "Why don't you write something for me to give them?"

That sounded like a terrible idea. But Kady found him an ink stand and a pen and a table to write on. And perhaps, he decided, it was better than sitting there trying to choke back tears that insisted on coming. He sat at the desk and thought. And wrote. And blotted and wrote again. The two hours it took to travel down the Ashley were gone as he folded his letter and handed it to Kady.

"As soon as I get back," she said. "I promise."

It was still a heavyhearted Austin who dragged himself down the gangplank in Charleston and along the pier to another boat, holding Jefferson by one hand and hauling his satchel in the other. At least his mother was strong enough now to carry her own bags and see to all the details she had never been able to take care of before.

But that was the only good thing he could think of. The rest of his thoughts were as gray as the wintry day. He refused to look out over the town. All he would see was the Charleston he'd never gotten to know.

The boat they went aboard was, to Austin's surprise, teeming with people, all of them women and children without Carolina accents.

"Is your husband a soldier here, too?" one woman asked Mother. "I haven't seen you before."

"No, we've just been visiting," Mother said.

Another woman poked her head in and pursed her lips. "I'll bet you're glad to cut that visit short," she said. "I'm so happy to get away from the hating eyes of these Southrons, I can't even tell you!"

Austin moved away, and this time he did stare sadly out the porthole at Charleston. Hating eyes? No. All he could see were the loving eyes of Charlotte, Henry-James, and Daddy Elias. And then he couldn't see anything, because a film covered everything.

It was beginning to grow dark by then anyway. Austin joined his mother and Jefferson in a corner and sat glumly in the dim light while the chatter of the military wives and their children went on around them.

"You're lucky," one of them said to Mother. "You're going *to* your husband. We're all going away from ours."

"They'll be home soon," someone else said. "If there is a war, it won't go on long. These Southrons think they're so clever, but Lincoln won't put up with their nonsense."

Austin searched in his pockets for something to stuff in his ears. He was tired of hearing it over and over.

Finally, they reached James Island, where Fort Johnson waved its Union flag in the last of the day's sun. When once again they navigated themselves down a gangplank, there was a tired-looking man with hollow cheeks and kind eyes waiting on shore. He held up his hand to try to silence the chittering of the wives and children.

"I am Major Robert Anderson," he said. "If you will give me your attention, ladies, please. Time is of the essence."

"What does that mean?" Jefferson whispered loudly.

"It means we have to hurry," Austin said. He could feel it in the air. Everyone there, including the soldiers who waited behind the major, seemed charged with tension. For the first time, he felt interested enough to listen.

"There has been a slight change of plans," Major Anderson said. "You are to be fetched by ship from Fort Sumter. Your husbands and the other soldiers are going to accompany you there and will remain at Fort Sumter after you've gone. We trust you will not mind sharing your accommodations with them across the harbor."

There was immediate chaos. Women snatched up their children and dashed to find their husbands. The island looked like an anthill, alive with frenzied families frantically scurrying for one more hour together and one more good-bye. Austin felt so alone that he grabbed Jefferson's hand without being told to and hung on.

"Mrs. Hutchinson?" a voice behind them said.

The three of them turned to see a young man, with well-toned muscles and ruddy hair and skin, smiling at them. He had eyes the green of mint tea and a lilting accent Austin wanted at once to ask about. But the young man was too much in charge to be asked any questions just then. As Mother nodded he took her arm firmly.

"You'll want to come with me," he said. "Your boat is waiting over here."

"My boat?" she said. She gave a little laugh. "I wasn't expecting any special treatment."

"Your husband said you were to be taken care of," he said.

Austin grinned suddenly. "You're Irish, aren't you?"

"I am, and proud of it. Fitzgerald Kearney's the name. Call me Fitz."

"Austin Hutchinson," Austin said, sticking out his hand.

Fitz shook it hurriedly. "Nice to meet you," he said. "But we'll have to take care of the formalities later. Right now, I've got to get you off this island."

Something in his voice made Austin grab Jefferson again and tow him quickly along behind Fitz and Mother. His heart started to race as the young man lifted her like a packet of feathers and deposited her aboard a small jolly boat Austin wasn't sure could make it all the way to Fort Sumter. His palms began to sweat despite the nippy cold.

"That's it, lads," Fitz said. "Take your seats and let's get on, then."

Austin peered through the darkness and just made out the hulking shape of Fort Sumter as Fitz took hold of the oars and deftly steered the little boat out into the harbor. The noise of

James Island quickly faded behind them. So did the fort.

"Aren't you going the wrong way?" Austin said, his heart nearly in his throat. "Fort Sumter's that way."

"We're not going to Fort Sumter, lad," Fitz said grimly. His smile was gone, and the muscles in his face were as tight as the ones in his arms.

"What do you mean?" Mother said. Her eyes lit up with alarm.

"I know what he means!" Austin cried. "We're being kidnapped!"

-⚓-⚓-⚓-

Chapter Seven

Sally Hutchinson drew herself up from the waist and tightened her frail fists. "I demand that you turn this boat around at once!"

Fitz didn't answer.

Mother sighed in exasperation. "That is ridiculous, isn't it? I can't any more demand anything of you than I can wrestle you to the ground!"

"No, Mrs. Hutchinson, you can't," Fitz said. He gave an almost devilish smile and kept rowing.

"I can!" Austin said. "Do you want me to take him on, Mother?"

Fitz tossed his head back and hooted. Austin knew his face was glowing red.

"That's all right, Austin," Mother said. Her voice was only a little shaky. "I'm sure we can reason with Mr. Kearney."

"There's no need to be afraid," Fitz said. "Honestly. I'm not kidnapping you, and I'm sure not going to hurt you."

"Then why won't you take us to Fort Sumter?" Austin said. "Didn't my father tell you to?"

"What's going on?" Jefferson said.

"I didn't exactly talk to your father, lad," Fitz said. "But I know he would—"

"You told us he *said* we were to get special treatment!" Austin cried.

"Austin!" Jefferson tugged at his sleeve. "What's happening? Where are we going?"

"I just have my orders," Fitz said.

"Who's giving you orders?" Austin said.

"Why is everybody yelling?" Jefferson said.

"Hush up, all of you!"

The males in the boat stared blankly at Sally Hutchinson. She stared them all down, and then she folded her hands in her lap.

"Now, then, gentlemen," she said, "let us start at the beginning. Mr. Kearney, who has given you orders to take us . . . wherever it is you're taking us?"

"Usually I only take orders from myself," Fitz said. Austin could see the gleam returning to his green eyes, even in the dark. "But of late I've been taking quite a few of them from a young lady you know."

"What young lady?" Austin said.

"Kady Ravenal," Fitzgerald said.

There was a second or two of silence before the boat seemed to explode with voices.

"Kady!"

"No!"

"How could you know Kady?"

"My cousin, Kady?"

"She'll explain all of that to you when she meets us at the dock," Fitz said.

"What dock?" Austin said.

Fitz pointed a rippling arm ahead. "That one—right there in Charleston."

"We're going back to Charleston?" Mother said. "I beg your

pardon, Mr. Kearney, but Kady would never put us in that kind of danger."

"You won't be in danger," he said. "We'll see that you get to safety."

"But we would have been perfectly safe on Fort Sumter, waiting for our ship to take us north," Mother said. She shook her head, so that several wisps of deer-colored hair fell down over her forehead. She was looking as confused as Austin felt.

"That's just it, Mrs. Hutchinson," Fitz said. "You wouldn't have been safe out there." He put up his hand. "And I'm going to let Kady explain that to you."

"If she's even there," Austin muttered.

He leaned forward and squinted into the night and stayed that way until Fitz paddled the boat up to a secluded dock. The silence of it against the backdrop of lively Charleston gave Austin chills.

But out of the darkness, a warm voice came down like a thick, welcoming blanket.

"Aunt Sally? Are you safe?" Kady said.

Jefferson could wait no longer. He sprang from the boat, rocking it to the side so that Austin had to hold on to keep from being dumped out into the harbor. Fitz lifted Mother out. Austin refused his hand and scrambled up onto the rickety dock, where Kady pulled them all into her arms.

"Come on," she said. "We have a wagon. We'll go to the townhouse."

Austin's head was full of questions, but he tucked them away—not too far—and hunkered down with his mother and brother under a blanket in the back of a waiting wagon. Jefferson was squealing with delight, but it was old hat to Austin by now. He'd spent one whole day hiding under a blanket.

The house on the East Battery was dark and cold until Fitz built a fire in the back sitting room and Kady handed out more blankets. Without the sparkling light of candles and oil lamps, the elegant place seemed less friendly than Henry-James's cabin. Austin shivered close to his mother until he was warm and until Jefferson was asleep with his head in her lap. Then he started asking questions. Kady had all the answers.

"The women and children of the soldiers were only being shipped to Fort Sumter as a cover for getting the soldiers themselves there," she said. "Major Anderson doesn't want the Southerners to know he's moving his men there, but he knows he'll be able to hold Fort Sumter more easily than he will Fort Johnson, if it does come to war."

"But won't the ship still come for the women and children?" Mother said. "Surely he doesn't mean for them to be out there if there's cannon fire?"

"There will be a ship eventually," Fitz said. "But it could be days, weeks, even months. You'd have been stuck out there."

"I'd much rather you were stuck here, with us," Kady said.

Austin wasn't the hugging kind, but he'd never wanted so much to throw his arms around somebody.

"We're staying a while then!" he said.

"Until another way can be figured out," Kady said.

Sally Hutchinson adjusted her blanket around her and cocked her head at Kady. "But what I don't understand, Kady, is how you knew all this. I'm completely baffled."

Austin wanted to know that, too. He watched closely as Kady and Fitz traded glances. The young man wiggled his eyebrows at her. Austin decided that was some kind of signal.

"I've learned all I know from Fitz," Kady said finally. "He's been a great help."

"And I appreciate that," Mother said. Her mouth twitched a little. "But how did you meet him, Kady? I can't imagine, with your mother hovering over you all the time."

"And how does *he* know?" Austin said, pointing to Fitz.

"We can't really tell you all that," Kady said. "It wouldn't be safe for anybody. But I promise you, we're not doing anything wrong."

"But you're doing something dangerous," Mother said. "That's what worries me."

Fitz turned from the fire with his eyes sharp. He stood up abruptly and whisked down a sword that was hanging decoratively in a scabbard above the fireplace. "I would never let anything happen to Kady, Mrs. Hutchinson," he said. "I'll stake my life on that!"

He swished the sword blade in a figure eight through the air, and then he leapt up onto a red wing chair, put one foot on its arm, and held the sword high over their heads.

"I pledge it on my life!" he cried out.

Jefferson woke up, blinking. Mother hugged him to her and stared. Austin looked around wildly for another weapon, though what he would have done with it, he hadn't a clue.

But Kady threw her handsome head back and howled.

"Fitzgerald Kearney, get down from there this instant! If my mother saw you, she'd whip that sword away from you and behead you with it. Don't you know that is a Gothic Victorian chair?"

Fitzgerald looked sheepishly at the chair he had his boots planted on and shrugged.

"A thousand pardons, madame," he said.

He jumped down, did one more irresistible swashbuckling move with the sword, and replaced it into its scabbard.

Jefferson clapped. His mother pushed his head back into her lap and told him to shush. Austin was still staring.

"How did you learn how to do that?" he said. "They haven't used that type of sword since the 1600s!"

"Ah, a clever boy, eh?" Fitz said. His green eyes gleamed. "We're behind the times in Ireland. We just *started* using them." He winked. "I'll teach you one day—"

"I think not," Mother said, still only half-laughing.

Austin got hastily to his knees. "You're not going to tell Uncle Drayton, are you, Mother?" he said. "I'm sure Fitz is all right."

"I don't know how else I'm going to explain why we're coming back to Canaan Grove!" she said.

"We have a whole boat ride to think of something," Kady said. "I assure you, Aunt Sally, we aren't doing anything wrong. I would never ask you to cover up a sin of mine, you know that."

"I do," Sally Hutchinson said without even hesitating. "I trust you as if you were my own daughter." She gave her head a sharp nod, sending more hair spilling over onto her forehead. "Good. When do we head back to Canaan Grove?"

"Right now," Fitz said. "I managed to delay your hired boat pilot."

Mother's mouth twitched. "I'm sure you did. What did you do, tie him to his mast?"

"Let's just say he's waiting for you—and I wouldn't wait until morning if I were you. The whole town is going to erupt when they find out Anderson has moved his men. No Northerner will be safe from their wrath."

Austin felt a tingle of excitement. Now that he was back to stay—for a while—the thought of dangerous adventure sounded delicious again.

And wait until I tell Charlotte about this one!

"Austin," Kady said as she pulled him up from his place on the floor, "this is just among us, you know. Please don't say anything to Charlotte about Fitz or any of this."

Austin felt himself sag. "Why not? You can trust her. You always tell her everything!"

"This is for her own safety," Kady said. "The less she knows, the less anyone can try to make her tell."

"Oh," Austin said.

"That's right," Kady said. "Oh."

Aunt Olivia sniffed when she got up the next morning and

discovered the Hutchinsons were back. She and Uncle Drayton spent an hour in the library, voices hot and muffled behind the door, and Austin could just imagine her stroking her double chins for all she was worth. The rest of them—Austin, Jefferson, Charlotte, Polly, and Tot—celebrated in Austin's mother's room with leftover gingerbread and hot chocolate.

"Now you don't have to miss any of the parties here, Boston," Polly said as she daintily cut the gingerbread into little pieces and passed it out. Jefferson, of course, popped his entire square into his mouth and begged for more.

"What parties?" Austin said.

"On the days following Christmas," she said primly, "there are always singing and dancing parties on the porch." She smiled at Tot. "The slaves, of course, have their own in the carpenter's shop."

"Those are the ones I want to go to," Austin said.

Polly sighed. "I might as well, too. We aren't going to have many guests coming here, that's for sure. It's as if the Ravenals have the plague now."

Austin suspected she rather liked that drama. It would give her something to swoon about when she *did* meet some boys. He could imagine her acting very courageous while she batted her eyelashes at them.

"What's all this, now?"

They all looked up to see Kady sweeping in, cheeks rosy, eyes glistening. Austin glanced quickly at Charlotte to see if she noticed it, too. It was going to be really hard to keep this secret from her.

"We're celebrating our reprieve," Mother said. "Come join us."

"What's a reprieve?" Jefferson asked.

Everyone looked at Austin.

"It's like a pardon," Austin said, licking some crumbs off his fingers.

"What's a pardon?" Jefferson said.

Austin ignored him as he watched Kady. She avoided everyone's eyes and sat on the bed next to her aunt.

"Are they yelling downstairs?" Charlotte said.

"Not anymore," Kady said. "Daddy is glad that the rumor was already about that the women and children might be stuck on Fort Sumter for months and that we got Aunt Sally and the boys back here. He says he'd much rather have you here." Her eyes sparkled at Austin.

So that was how she explained it, he thought.

"Mama is not so happy," Kady went on, "but she's getting over it quickly."

"Why?" Austin said. He leaned in. "What do you know?"

She stretched out on the bed with her hands behind her head, eyes still dancing. "How much is it worth to you?"

"I'll give you all the rose water I've made!" Polly said at once.

"I'll brush your hair for you!" Charlotte said.

Mother nudged Kady. "I won't give you anything. Just tell!"

"I know that Daddy has decided that if he is going to—how did he put it?—'save the South from itself,' he is going to have to remain loyal to it."

"What does that mean?" Polly said. She shook her limp curls impatiently. "Speak English, Kady!"

"It means that he is going to Charleston for the social season and he is going to get back his influence there so he can keep South Carolina from killing itself."

"I don't understand," Austin said. "Has he changed his mind? Is he glad South Carolina seceded now?"

Kady shook her head. "No, but he thinks if he goes along with it, they'll start listening to him again and he can talk them out of going to war. We have to be in Charleston for him to do that."

Polly sat bolt upright, a piece of gingerbread half-eaten in her hand. "Are we all going?" she said.

"Yes," Kady said. "All of us. Even Aunt Sally and the boys."

"Are you sure?" Mother said.

"Positive. Daddy said he doesn't see how he can leave you out here. You're much safer under the same roof with him where he can keep an eye on you until Uncle Wesley finds another way to get you home. And if we do get word from him, you'll already be in Charleston where you'll be taking your leave."

Charlotte clapped her hands, grabbed Austin by the arm, let go, and clapped again. Then she started to giggle—and didn't stop. Austin stared at her for a minute before he turned back to Kady.

"Will we have to hide in the house all the time?"

Kady grinned, earlobe to earlobe. "This is the best part," she said. "You won't be allowed to go anywhere without Henry-James so he can protect you."

Austin squawked, and this time *he* grabbed *Charlotte's* arm. They got up and started to dance on the bed, but Mother shouted them down and chased them out, laughing herself.

"I can't believe it!" Charlotte squealed as they tore down the steps to go and tell Daddy Elias.

Austin wasn't sure he believed it either. Only later, when Austin was trying to calm down enough to get to sleep, did he think of something.

It was Jesus, of course, he thought. *Getting me through that narrow gate.*

He sighed and started to drift off, but not before it came to him that this wouldn't be the last gate he'd have to squeeze through. He'd better talk to Jesus—a lot.

The next few days were a flurry of activity as the Ravenals and Hutchinsons prepared to leave for Charleston. Polly and Aunt Olivia were frantic that they wouldn't have enough clothes for all the concerts, ballets, and balls that were on the agenda. Aunt Olivia wrote up invitations for a masquerade ball at the townhouse and started planning her and Kady's costumes, Uncle Drayton buttoned up the plantation for his departure, and Charlotte and Austin spent their time saying good-bye to the people who were going to be left behind.

Bogie seemed to know they were leaving and spent his time going from one of them to the other in the cabin, sighing and slobbering on their hands.

"They be back 'fore you knows it," Daddy Elias said to the dog.

"I don't know if I will be back," Austin said. "We're taking everything we brought, just in case—"

"Don't you worry 'bout that none," Daddy Elias said. "I's gonna see you again. I can jus' feel it."

Austin waited while Daddy Elias coughed and tried to catch his breath.

"When am I going to get where I can just 'feel' things?" he said.

"You jus' keep on talkin' to Marse Jesus," Daddy Elias said. "You gonna get there."

"Through a narrow gate," Austin said.

Daddy Elias nodded, and then he coughed some more.

But Austin wasn't convinced. You obviously had to be something very special before that could happen. You had to be brave and independent like Kady or spectacular like Fitz or wise like Daddy Elias or just plain good like Mother and Charlotte.

And I'm not any of those, Austin thought. *I thought it was all right just to be who I was—but now I'm not so sure about that. Not with all these narrow gates in front of me.*

The next day—January first—they had ham biscuits and Hoppin' John soup to start the new year. It was Austin's first taste of black-eyed peas. He hoped they didn't have those in Charleston.

He was about to find out. The next morning they set out for

the city, and this time he didn't have to hide in a coil of rope or write a good-bye letter. It was a time full of anticipation, rewarded when they reached the elegant townhouse once again, where everything was 10 times more grand even than the plantation Big House.

With its wide porches on all three stories and its pale-yellow sides shining in the sunlight, it was easily the most impressive house on the East Battery. It was Austin's first chance to really explore it all, and that he did with Charlotte, from the dormered attic to the glorious garden, complete with their new joggling board.

When they had pulled every bell pull and climbed up and down every stairway, Austin was ready to take on Charleston itself. It took some persuading, but they were finally able to convince Uncle Drayton that Henry-James would not let them out of his sight, especially Austin.

"And if you see the first sign of Virgil Rhett or Lawson Chesnut or Roger Pryor, you get out of the way at once," Uncle Drayton said.

Austin didn't need any convincing. He'd had enough fruit thrown at him to last a lifetime.

Uncle Drayton had a two-seated buggy that only required one horse. Henry-James took them out in that, and Austin decided right then that maybe he would be a city dweller instead of a country gentleman when he was older. He even wished for a minute that he had a fancy bowler hat like some of the men he saw.

But he forgot about clothes the instant they were in the thick of the city. His head twisted back and forth as if it were on a spring as he tried to take in the things he hadn't seen before. Charlotte could hardly keep up with answers to his questions.

"That's the Customs House. . . . That's the Vanderhorst House—it has apartments—the first ones in America. . . . There's St. Michael's Church . . . St. Phillips . . . First Presbyterian—"

By the time they reached the Mills House, Austin was convinced this was the best city in the world. Sure, it was backward compared to the towns in the North, where they already had running water and gaslights in the houses. Still, with its tile roofs and old graveyards and cobblestone streets, it was almost enchanting.

But the fairy tale faded as they were brought to a halt in front of the hotel. Someone was on an upper balcony, making a speech to a crowd in the street below. The listeners were roaring and cheering at the end of every sentence, just the way they had the night of the secession. It made Austin's chest ache again.

"We have a duty!" the southern man was shouting. "South Carolina has a duty to take arms again the detested Constitution. We must protect ourselves from its outrageous injustices!"

Charlotte tugged nervously at Austin's sleeve. "Is he talking about war?" she said.

"Soldiers, sailors," the orator cried, "resign your Union commissions and join the Confederate military!"

"He is!" Charlotte whispered. "Henry-James, take us home."

"I's tryin, Miz Lottie," Henry-James said. He looked helplessly at the knot of traffic stopped in the road by the speech.

Suddenly, there was an outburst from the corner. The crowd turned as if it had one head, and even the speaker stopped shouting.

"What's happening over there?" Charlotte said. "Austin, this is scaring me!"

Austin got up on his knees to look. It appeared that some men were burning something in one of the barrels on the corner of Meeting and Market Streets.

"What is it?" someone in the crowd shouted. "What are you burning?"

One of the men waved a handful of pamphlets, which he

tossed into the flames. "Abolitionist tracts," he said. "Traitor literature!"

Once again the crowd cheered.

"Let us help!" one man called out. "Toss some here!"

The men needed no encouragement. At once they flung stacks of the pamphlets, until the sky was momentarily filled with over-sized confetti. The hated little anti-slavery booklets showered down, even into the buggy.

Charlotte caught one and handed it to Austin.

"What does it say, Boston?" she said.

Austin stared at the front of the booklet, and he was sure his chest was going to split open.

"It says, '*The Evils of Slavery*, by Wesley Hutchinson.' "

Austin swallowed and looked at Henry-James.

"You better take us back to the house, Henry-James," he said. "And fast."

✝ ✜ ✝

Chapter Eight

T he ladies were having tea in the front sitting room that overlooked the harbor when Charlotte and Austin burst in. Aunt Olivia looked up from the little cracker spread with something gray that she was about to put into her mouth and drew her lips up into an annoyed knot that drew her chins in with it.

"What is it?" she said. "Can I not enjoy a pâté de foie gras without you children interrupting with one of your silly crises?"

"This one isn't silly," Austin said, and added, "ma'am."

Aunt Olivia sniffed and offered a plate to Polly. "Biscuit glacé?" she said.

"Merci," Polly said.

Austin groaned inside. What a time to practice their French.

But Kady got up and came over to him, and her eyes were full of questions.

"Are you two all right?" she said. "What happened out there?"

Austin poured out the story while Charlotte nodded confirmation at Kady's side. As Austin talked, Mother's face grew more and more grim.

"I told Drayton this was not going to work," Aunt Olivia said, still nibbling at her pâté.

"It will work, Mama," Kady said. "We're just going to have to be very careful."

"Henry-James took good care of us," Austin said quickly. "I don't think we have to stay inside all the time."

"That isn't what I'm worried about," Mother said. "It's the nights that frighten me."

"Who's frightened?" Uncle Drayton said from the doorway.

Once again they told the story. He nodded, frowning, for a minute, and then he slapped his hands together as if he had had a brilliant idea.

"Suppose we move some cots for the boys into your room, Sally?" he said. "And then I'll have Henry-James sleep right outside your door. That way you'll feel completely safe, and you can get your rest. You're looking puny again to me. How does that sound?"

"I like it!" Austin said.

"As if it were up to you to decide," Aunt Olivia said. "Now then, Drayton, what do you say to salmon for dinner, and perhaps some English grouse?"

"I won't eat a heavy meal before the party," Polly said. "I'll never get into my gown."

"I hope it isn't a somber affair," Aunt Olivia said fretfully.

"Everyone seems to be trying to stay cheerful," Uncle Drayton said. "I had a pleasant luncheon with James Pettigru, the judge, you know—"

"But it's as if there were a cloud hanging over our heads," Aunt Olivia said. "Mrs. Singleton came to call on me this morning. She agrees it's hard to settle down to anything when one's heart is in one's mouth all the time. And the air is hot with rumors. She said that—"

Charlotte gave Austin a poke, and they retreated into the hall.

"It's going to be all right," she whispered to him.

"I think so," Austin said.

But he couldn't get a few hot things of his own out of his head, even when he and Charlotte were playing on the joggling board or chasing Jefferson through the garden or sitting on their beds in his mother's room at night while she read to them. The thoughts were always burning.

What is *the secret that Henry-James and Kady have?*

How does *Kady know all the things she and Fitz know about what's happening in Charleston?*

Am I going to be able to keep this from Charlotte?

What if they're all in some kind of trouble? Won't they need my help? What if Father sends for us before I know? Before I'm finished here?

It was overwhelming. He tried to pray—but there were no answers.

"You be a person Marse Jesus gonna be proud to know," Daddy Elias had always said, "and Marse Jesus gonna get the truth to you on time."

But where was the "feeling" the old man always said he had? All Austin felt was anxious—right in the middle of his chest.

One thing *was* good. Over the next few days, Aunt Olivia seemed to discover that Charlotte and Austin were actually quite useful. She fell into the habit of sending them on errands . . . so Mousie could stay by her side and hand her handkerchiefs and things.

One morning, so early the milk wagon hadn't even creaked up the drive yet, Aunt Olivia swept into the dining room where they were having breakfast and thrust a scented envelope into Austin's hand.

"I need for you to take this to Mary Chesnut," she said. "She's staying at the Mills House. I want to invite her for tea."

Austin grinned across the table at Charlotte. "Yes, ma'am, right away," he said. "As soon as I finish my waffles."

"You've had plenty," she said, whisking away his plate. "You run on now—and comb your hair first. I won't have you embarrassing me with that cowlick."

Across the table, Kady rolled her eyes. But just then the bell rang at the front door and her face formed a serious expression. She scraped her chair back and hurried out of the dining room.

"We have slaves to answer doors!" Aunt Olivia called after her. She clicked her tongue. "I might as well give up on that girl. She will never turn into a lady."

"Don't give up on *me*, Mama," Polly said. "I'm a lady."

"Yes, you are, my pet," Aunt Olivia said.

Austin glanced at Charlotte, who gave him a look that said, "I think I'm going to be sick!"

Austin chewed his last mouthful of waffle and left the dining room to get his hat. In the hallway, he bumped into Kady.

"Who was at the door?" he said.

"Nosy little fella, aren't you?" she said. "It was just someone delivering a ham."

"To the front door?" Austin said.

But Kady brushed on by, and Austin went for his hat, rejoicing with Charlotte on his way out the door.

It was a crisp, clear day, and Austin felt alive and eager for something different to do as Henry-James set the horse to clopping its hooves down Meeting Street. He liked hearing the calls from the market as they passed, the Pepper Sauce Man calling, "Pure Jamaica pepper sauce! Fresh red pepper sauce!" and the Oyster Man crying, "Shuckin' time! Two fresh pounds, just a dime!"

He also laughed until he thought he'd pass out when Henry-James turned around to Charlotte and said, "Miz Lottie, close your eyes and open your hands. I gots a special Christmas gif' for you."

When Charlotte did, Henry-James deposited a slimy oyster in her hands. Charlotte squealed—and then waited for Henry-James to turn around again so she could slide it down his back.

But that wasn't quite enough to keep Austin interested. He had the lay of the land in his head now. It was time for an adventure.

"What shall we do, Henry-James?" he said.

"Stay out of trouble," Henry-James said over his shoulder.

"You're not as much fun since you became responsible," Austin said.

Henry-James gave a good-natured grunt and pulled the carriage up to the Mills House.

"Y'all don't get into nothin' while I takes this message in here," he said. "You hear me?"

They nodded innocently. The minute he was gone, they were both up on their knees, looking around. Austin, of course, was careful to keep his hat somewhat over his eyes, but no one appeared to be looking for abolitionists' sons.

Suddenly, Charlotte pinched his arm.

"Austin!" she hissed. "There's Kady!"

Austin was at once uneasy. "So?"

"But look! Look where she's going!"

Austin had no choice but to look. He was just in time to see Kady disappearing into the alley in a buggy. She was driving it herself.

"That wasn't Daddy's buggy," Charlotte said. "What is she doing?"

Austin tried to look casual. "I don't know," he said, shrugging. "Isn't that her business?"

Charlotte turned to stare at him. Her mouth even hung open. "Austin Hutchinson, I don't believe I'm hearing this!" she said. "Not five minutes ago, you said you wanted an adventure."

"I do, but this isn't an adventure."

"Of course it is!"

Henry-James reappeared and climbed into the little seat in

front of them. Before he could even pick up the reins, Charlotte said, "Henry-James, go down that alley! We're going to follow Kady!"

Henry-James looked as if he'd been shot.

"Miz Kady?" he said. "I don't see no Miz Kady."

"Of course you don't!" Charlotte said. "She's gone down the alley, and if you don't hurry, we'll lose her!"

"Maybe she want to be lost, Miz Lottie," Henry-James said.

"What is the matter with you two?" Charlotte fairly shrieked. "Any other day, you would be telling *me* it would be fun to go after her. Come on!"

Henry-James sighed and urged the horse on. "All right, Miz Lottie," he said. "Whatever you say."

Austin wished he hadn't said that. But there didn't seem to be anything they could do but careen around the corner into the alley and set their sights for Kady.

Her buggy had turned down East Bay Street by the time they got a clear view of her again. Charlotte told Henry-James to hang back so she wouldn't see them.

"I don't think it matters," Austin said. "It looks like she's heading for the house."

But just then, Kady whipped the buggy down a little side street, toward the harbor. The wharf was crowded with slaves carrying barrels on their shoulders and fishermen selling boiled crayfish in smelly buckets, so it was easy to blend in with the hubbub. Kady, however, didn't seem interested in anything else but getting to the dock. Austin's chest was burning like there was a bonfire blazing in there.

"All right, we followed her—we know where she went," he said. "We should go home."

"Who's that?" Charlotte said, pointing.

Austin looked, and groaned to himself. Hurrying toward the buggy was Fitzgerald Kearney. Austin would have recognized his muscled arms and his ruddy hair anywhere. Together, he and Kady opened the baggage carrier on the back of the buggy and lifted out a trunk. Whatever was in it was heavy, because Kady's slender back bent over like a willow branch as she took her end.

"You done seen enough, Miz Lottie?" Henry-James said. He was licking his lips fast and hard, and his neck looked stiff.

He knows *what she's doing!* Austin thought suddenly. *This is part of their secret!*

Charlotte was watching Kady as if she were in a trance. Together with Fitz, Kady carried the trunk up the gangplank of a small, two-masted ketch, the kind Austin knew was usually used for cargo and fishing. Attached to its stern was a jolly boat for excursions into shore that looked familiar to Austin.

"We can go now," Charlotte said, her voice low. "I don't want Kady to see us."

As they made their way away from the wharf and back onto East Bay Street, all the excitement vanished from Charlotte's face. She was quiet, almost sad-looking.

"I think Kady is in some kind of trouble," she said. "I felt like I was watching somebody who wasn't my sister."

"Maybe you were just surprised," Austin said carefully.

"But who was that young man she was with? She isn't allowed to keep company with boys without a chaperone, you know."

"I don't think they were out there courting," Austin said.

"What *do* you think they were doing?"

Austin couldn't even venture a guess. Out of the corner of his eye, he saw Henry-James getting stiffer and stiffer. He knew more than he was saying, that was clear.

"I think we should keep our eyes open," Charlotte said.

Austin tried not to shift in his seat. "For what?" he said.

"I don't know—just in case Kady needs our help. We've always been able to help before, haven't we?"

Her eyes were pleading as she looked at Austin. He was afraid she was going to start crying again. There had been enough tears lately.

"Yes, we have," he said. He nodded and tried to smile. "We can keep our eyes open. Who knows, right?"

"Right!" she said. And she looked a little happier again.

Austin changed the subject to the Georgian-style house they passed on South Battery that he'd heard had been built by a cousin of George Washington's who had also fought in the American Revolution.

"Is it true he had no flag for his command at the Battle of Eutaw Springs?" Austin said. "So his bride made him one from her mother's curtains?"

Nobody knew, but it lifted the cloud from over their heads for at least a little while.

Kady, it seemed, was much better at keeping secrets than they could ever dream of being. While Charlotte kicked Austin under the table every time Kady came into the room, Kady herself went about her business as if everything were completely normal and she *weren't* running about behind everyone's back with a swashbuckling young Irishman with bright green eyes and wiggling eyebrows. In fact, that very night, when all the children were piled onto the beds in Austin's mother's room, Kady breezed in with some tiny canapés she'd brought home from a party and plopped herself down in the midst of them like she did any other night. Charlotte could hardly keep her eyes from popping out, Austin could tell.

"Where have you been, Miss Kady?" Mother said.

"I walked home from the party," Kady said. "It was deadly dull. All anyone can talk about is stomping the Yankees. Taste one of these—they're ham."

"I'm glad I wasn't there, then," Mother said. "I'd much rather spend my time with you children, anyway."

"Read to us, Aunt Sally, please," Charlotte said.

Mother opened *A Tale of Two Cities*, which Austin had already read. As her voice eased on through the pages, Austin thought back over the day, and soon his eyes grew heavy.

When they opened, the room was dark. The only sounds came from his mother and Jefferson breathing evenly in their sleep . . . and someone at Mother's dressing table.

Sleepily, Austin came up on his elbow and peered through the shadows. The shutters had been left open a crack, and the moon made a trail through it. In its light, he could see a slender figure in front of the looking glass.

It looked like Kady, except that her thick hair was cascading down her back, and Kady always wore her hair up in a chignon at the back of her neck. But even as he watched, the girl appeared to be wrapping something into a small tube shape. It crackled like a piece of paper.

And then she tucked it into her hair and with nimble fingers rolled the whole thing up into the usual knot at the nape of her neck.

It *was* Kady—Kady putting the hairpins in place, Kady taking up the cape she'd left lying across the chair and wrapping it around herself, Kady sneaking out the door in the middle of the night.

Charlotte was right, Austin thought. *Kady is in big trouble.*

✛ ◆ ✛

ustin could barely stay inside his own skin, much less remain in bed. He climbed from beneath the covers and slipped out into the hall. Henry-James was sleeping on a pallet against the wall, and he flinched when Austin shook him.

" 'Scuse me for sayin', Massa Austin," he said in a sleep-thick voice, "but what's so important you gots to wake me up now?"

But when Austin told him, he sprang up like it was noontime and groped for his shoes.

"What are you doing?" Austin said.

"I gots to follow her," Henry-James said.

"You do? Why?"

" 'Cause I promised Miz Lottie I'd keep an eye on Miz Kady."

"But won't you get in trouble with Uncle Drayton for leaving your post here?"

Henry-James wriggled into the jacket of his livery uniform. "If'n I gots to make a choice between Marse Drayton and Miz Lottie, that's like no choice at all."

Austin took a moment to be impressed. Last fall, he'd seen what Uncle Drayton could do when he was angry with a slave. If Henry-James was willing to risk getting beaten or sold, he was the bravest person Austin knew. And doing something brave certainly sounded better than staying behind and jumping at every noise.

You see? Austin said to himself. *Everybody else knows what to do.*

"I'm going with you," Austin whispered. "And don't argue with me."

"I wasn't goin' to, Massa Austin," Henry-James said.

The two of them crept out of the house and stood on the East Battery until they could make out a dark figure in a trailing cape disappearing toward the wharves. They ducked in and out of the shadows and zigzagged from tree to tree until she vanished inside a warehouse.

"C'mon," Henry-James whispered.

They, too, found the warehouse door, but when Austin put his hand on the doorknob, Henry-James shook his head and pointed to a window. They wiped the dirt off it with their hands and peered inside.

Kady was there, standing between a trunk and Fitz, unrolling her hair. Austin watched for the tube of paper, which indeed fell out. Fitz took it up and nodded his head, as if he were beckoning someone from the shadows. The silhouette of a slender black boy appeared.

"Who's that?" Austin whispered.

"Somebody's slave," Henry-James whispered back. "See them whip marks 'cross his leg?"

Austin did, and he shuddered. He would never get used to slave masters beating their people.

Fitz was busily tucking the piece of paper into a small pack that he fastened to the slave's back. Kady opened the trunk, and the slave boy stepped inside. Fitz fastened the clasps, and then he stood up. Wiggling his eyebrows, he grabbed Kady, dipped her backward, and looked as if he were going to—ugh!—kiss her.

Austin turned his head and plastered his hands over his eyes. "Good grief!" he said.

But Henry-James grabbed his arm and gave it a tug.

"C'mon, Massa Austin," he said. "We gots to hide 'fore they comes out. We seen enough."

"You know what they're up to, don't you?" Austin said as Henry-James nearly carried him away from the warehouse.

"Miz Kady tol' me some," Henry-James said. "I just had to see for myself. But I can't tell Miz Lottie."

"No, you can't," Austin said. "We just have to pretend this never happened."

"Let's get on home," Henry-James said.

But before they could take another step, the warehouse door creaked open. Henry-James grew wild-eyed for a second, but Austin looked around. The only hiding place he saw was a wagon, drawn up to the corner of the warehouse.

"There!" he whispered to Henry-James.

They skittered to it like a pair of squirrels and wriggled under a blanket. Blankets in wagons were beginning to feel like home to Austin.

He was about to lift a corner and peek out when he realized the footsteps of Kady and Fitz were getting closer to them, not farther away.

"They're coming here!" Austin squeaked.

Henry-James nudged him and grew so still that Austin wondered if he were breathing. He held his own breath and waited.

From the fair amount of grunting Kady was doing, it sounded as if they were loading the trunk right onto the wagon. Once it was thudded into place, Austin could hear them climbing up into the driver's seat and Fitz clicking his tongue at the horse. With a lurch, they were moving. Austin breathed, but not too easily.

"We'll get out when they stop," he whispered to Henry-James.

From the smell of sea air, Austin knew they were going toward the wharves. He could hear the thick lines that held the ships to their docks creaking as the vessels rocked on the water. The wagon stopped, Kady and Fitz climbed down, and they at once slid the trunk out of the wagon.

"I've got it, love," they heard Fitz say.

"Glory, you're strong," Kady said.

"Can we get out now, do you think?" Austin whispered to Henry-James.

There was no answer. There was only a sudden blast of cold as the blanket was whipped off them.

"What on earth?" Kady said. "What are you two doing here? I thought I told you *both*—"

"Halt! Who goes there?"

It was another voice, not Fitz's. It stopped three hearts as it blared out through the night. Kady let the blanket fall back over the boys.

"Top of the evenin' to ya," Kady called back to the voice.

Austin gasped, and Henry-James gave him a poke.

She's talking with an Irish accent! Austin thought. *Why is she doing that?*

"And just what are you doin' here in the middle of the night?" the big voice said as it drew nearer.

"Ah, and you'd be the watchman, eh?" Kady said, still trilling the brogue.

"I am, and I want to know who *you* would be."

"My name's Katherine," she said. "Katherine O'Brien."

"That doesn't explain what you're doing out here."

"Why, I'm waitin' for my ship to come in," she said, as if she were saying, "I'm breathing."

"There won't be any ships comin' in here until dawn!" the man said.

Kady giggled—something Kady never did. "I know," she said. "I'm such a silly lass. I'm just so afraid I'm goin' to miss it, you know. With all the talk of war here, I just want to get back to Ireland before the shootin' starts."

The man grunted. "I can't say I blame you," he said. "I wish I had someplace to run off to. Silliest thing I ever heard of."

"Aye, that it is."

"Is he with you?" the watchman said. "That one comin' from the harbor?"

Austin caught his breath.

"Aye, he is. That's my brother," Kady said. "I made him carry our trunk all the way to the end of the dock so we'd be the first ones on."

"Well, you can't spend the night here," the watchman said. "Take your wagon to White Point Garden there, at the end of the Battery. I see you've got some blankets. You'll be warm enough."

"Thank you kindly," Kady said.

Austin could hear the watchman's footsteps fading and Fitz's approaching. No one said a word as the wagon rocked with their getting on. Only when the sounds of the sea were behind them did Kady whisper hoarsely, "We're taking you two ruffians back to the house."

Austin finally relaxed, though Henry-James remained stiff as a fence post.

I know two things for sure now, Austin thought. *Kady is helping Fitz smuggle slaves out of the South. And she's in love with him.*

Love wasn't something Austin thought about much, not the boy-girl kind of love Polly was always going on about. He and Charlotte agreed that that was strictly for other people, not them.

He'd always thought Kady felt that way, too. She certainly wasn't interested in any of the beaus Aunt Olivia had provided for her.

Fitz is strong and handsome, Austin thought. *And definitely brave. But I don't think Aunt Olivia and Uncle Drayton are going*

to be too happy about this if they find out. He isn't exactly the
upper-crust gentleman of Charleston they had in mind. He
stands on chairs waving swords!

When the wagon stopped, Kady pulled back the blanket. Austin looked up at her sheepishly. Henry-James looked as if he were going to be sick.

"Oh, stop it, you two," Kady said. "I'm not mad at you. I should have known your curiosities would kill you. You can never leave anything alone."

Austin sat up and saw that they were indeed at White Point Garden, a few blocks from the house.

"We'll walk from here," she said. "Hop on out now."

They did. Austin was careful not to look back, just in case she and Fitz were kissing again.

Kady caught up to them quickly and tucked her arms through theirs as they made their way toward the townhouse.

"All right," she said. "Ask your questions. I know you have thousands of them."

Henry-James didn't say anything. Austin said plenty.

"Are you smuggling slaves out?" he said.

"Yes. When Mama sent me into Charleston for those few weeks in the fall for French lessons, I saw Fitz in the Market Place, and he treated the slaves so kindly, as if they were people."

"Just like you does, Miz Kady," Henry-James said.

"Thank you," she said. "I try. And I knew this was a person I had to meet. So . . . I did."

"Aunt Olivia would have a fit if she knew," Austin said.

"Wouldn't she, though? I can just imagine her face turning purple. Anyway, when Fitz confided in me what he was doing, I had to be a part of it. I was so afraid we weren't going to come to Charleston for the season, so I'm in heaven." She looked at Austin sideways. "That is, if you can keep a secret."

"Of course!"

"It won't be easy," she said. "I didn't want you to know this much so you wouldn't have to lie or sneak around. I know how you try to do what's right." She shrugged. "But you did make the choice to find out what I was doing. Now you have to carry it on your shoulders. If you don't, people like Henry-James could suffer."

"I can carry it, then!" Austin said. "Only—"

She stopped them at the gate to the house and squinted at Austin. "Only what?" she said. "There can't be any 'onlies' in this, you know."

"I wish we could tell Charlotte," Austin said. "It just doesn't seem fair, us knowing and her being in the dark."

Kady thought for a moment, and then she sighed. "You might as well tell her," she said. "She's already followed me once."

Henry-James's eyes flickered fear at Austin. Austin himself stammered.

"Oh, stop it," Kady said. "I saw the three of you, trying to be so sly while you trailed me in your buggy." She shook her head. "Don't ever try to be spies."

"So we can tell her?" Austin said.

Kady nodded. Then she leaned against the gate. "Any more questions? We may not have a chance to talk about all this again. It isn't safe, you know."

Austin did have some. They surprised him as they popped into his mind.

"I want the slaves free, too," he said. "But is this right, what you're doing?"

"I thought about it a great deal," she said. "All those times I would go off by myself and write poetry. All the time I spent talking to Aunt Sally—it was all I could think about and talk about. And here's what I've decided." She swallowed and got herself ready. "We must abolish slavery. If that means robbing the slave masters, then I am proud to be called a thief."

"But don't thieves get punished?" Austin said.

"They do. We're breaking the southern law, after all. If we're caught, we'd probably be put in prison. But I believe that everyone, black or white, should defy the law when the law is wrong. In fact, we're so busy helping slaves escape, we don't have time to argue about the right of our cause." She smiled with a dreamy look in her eyes. "That's what Fitz says."

"My father always says," Austin said quickly, before the conversation could get too mushy, "that prejudice against color is a rebellion against God."

Kady nodded. "I wish I had a chance to get to know Uncle Wesley," she said. "I could learn so much from him."

"You plenty smart already, Miz Kady," Henry-James said.

It was the first thing he'd said in a while, and Austin suddenly looked at him sharply. *Why had Kady already told him all about the slave smuggling? And hadn't their secret started before she even came to Charleston and met Fitz?*

He didn't ask, though. Kady hustled them both into the house and made sure they got to Austin's mother's room without being caught.

But being in his bed and going to sleep were two entirely different things. Austin lay awake for hours, thinking, praying, practicing what he was going to say to Charlotte.

The practice paid off. When he told her the next morning after breakfast, she got up from the joggling board and marched straight to Kady, who was sitting with her notebook on the upper piazza.

"I want to help," Charlotte said to her sister.

Kady put down her pen, and her face twitched. Austin wasn't sure whether she was trying not to laugh or trying not to cry.

"Austin's told you," she said.

"Yes," Charlotte said. And again she said, "I want to help."

Austin found himself staring at her. Where had shy, uncertain little Charlotte gone?

"If there is any way I see that you *and* Austin can help me, I will surely tell you," Kady said. "As long as I think it can be done with no harm to you."

That was good enough for Charlotte. And it got the wheels and the prayers going in Austin's busy head . . . which was a good thing, because the opportunity arose sooner than anyone ever dreamed it would.

✢ ❖ ✢

harlotte and Austin's chance came just a few days later, when preparations for Aunt Olivia's masquerade ball were in full swing. Mousie and Tot were busily polishing brass and scrubbing floors, and Josephine was preparing she-crab soup and Huguenot torte and some kind of quail dish that made Austin's mouth water every time he passed through the kitchen building.

Aunt Olivia, of course, was fussing over whether to wear spool-heeled shoes with her Spanish lady costume or just slippers. Kady was enduring her final fitting into her replica of a gown Queen Elizabeth once wore, rolling her eyes the entire time.

"I don't see what you're fuming about," Polly said as she watched the seamstress slave pinch in the dress at Kady's slim waist. She stuck out her thin lower lip. "I would give anything to be going to this party."

"Now, Polly," Aunt Olivia said, still examining the spool-heeled shoes, "we've been over this a thousand times. This party is not appropriate for you. Next year, perhaps."

Polly sniffed. "I would look so fine in that costume."

"Believe me, Polly," Kady said, "I would gladly give it to you—mask, wig, and all."

Aunt Olivia pulled her chin in so far that it looked like she had three of them. "Kady Sarah, you hush now. You are going to meet some nice young man tonight who is going to sweep you right off your feet."

Charlotte and Austin glanced at each other doubtfully. Kady shot them a warning look.

When the bell rang at the door, they both dashed toward it.

"Good," Aunt Olivia called after them. "Make yourselves useful. You're underfoot today!"

Austin opened the door to a fit-looking man in a messenger's uniform who had gray hair and eyebrows and whiskers.

"Top o' the mornin'," he said. "I've a message for Miss Kady Ravenal. From Miss Orlis's School for Young Ladies."

"What school?" Austin said, looking dubiously at the envelope the Irishman held out to him.

"That's where she went for French lessons in the fall," Charlotte said. "We'll give it to her."

"See that you do, eh?" the messenger said. He handed the envelope to Austin.

When he took it, Austin couldn't help noticing the man's hands. They were firm and ruddy, not pale and gnarled the way the hands of an old man with whiskers should look.

Austin looked up at him quickly, but the Irishman gave his gray eyebrows a wiggle, lowered his hat over his eyes—his green eyes—and hurried away.

"What's the matter, Boston?" Charlotte whispered as she closed the door.

"That was Fitzgerald Kearney, in disguise," Austin whispered back. "This is a message from him!"

Charlotte's eyes sparked excitement. "We have to sneak it to her!"

"How are we going to do that without Aunt Olivia sticking her nose in?"

As if she'd been waiting for a cue, Aunt Olivia chose that moment to shriek from the drawing room, "Char-lotte!"

Charlotte squeezed her face shut, but Austin poked her.

"Yes, Mama?" she said.

"Go upstairs and get Kady's gloves. I want to see what the entire costume looks like all together."

"That's it!" Austin hissed. "Go get them!"

Charlotte charged up the stairs, petticoats flying, while Austin waited impatiently at the bottom. When she returned with a pair of fingerless, elbow-length mittens made of ecru lace, Austin took a second to frown at them.

"They didn't wear gloves like this in Queen Elizabeth's time," he whispered.

"Never mind that! Hurry!" Charlotte said. "What's your idea?"

Austin folded the envelope into a tiny half and fitted it neatly into one of the gloves.

"When she puts it on, she'll feel that in her palm," Austin said. "Kady's good at all this. She'll know what to do."

"I hope so," Charlotte said. "I would hate to ruin anything for her."

Austin let Charlotte take the gloves in and waited outside the room. He could only take so much of Aunt Olivia's fussing and Polly's whining. When Charlotte came out, her cheeks were flushed.

"She felt it!" she whispered. "I could see it in her eyes."

It wasn't two minutes later when Kady herself emerged into the hallway and, closing the door behind her, ripped off the glove and tore open the envelope. Austin watched her lips move silently as she read and saw her eyes grow bigger with every word.

"What is it?" Charlotte said. "What does it say?"

Kady glanced over her shoulder. Then she moved the children

into the music room, which was for the moment polished and empty and waiting for the party guests.

"It's from Fitz," she whispered, so low that Austin could barely hear her. "He says tonight is our chance. He has the preacher and the chapel and everything."

"Your chance?" Charlotte said. "For what?"

"To get married," Kady said.

Charlotte gasped so loudly that Austin had to clap his hand over her mouth. Kady looked around again with a sort of panicky glow in her eyes.

"It may be our only chance for a long time," she said. "Especially if a war starts."

"So are you going to sneak out and do it?" Austin asked.

Charlotte's eyes bugged out. "Just go out and get married? What about a wedding? What about the slaves rowing you up the river—and your dress and the cake—"

"I don't care about any of that," Kady said, almost fiercely. "I just want to be Fitz's wife. And you know Mama and Daddy would never give me a wedding to marry someone without money."

"So go do it," Austin said. "We'll help you."

"This isn't a game, Austin," Kady said. "This is very serious."

"I know," Austin said. And he did. He had never felt more serious in his life. It seemed like it was time for people to do what they could do before the black cloud that seemed to be hanging over them burst and washed away all their hopes for happiness. This looked like a narrow gate, and he wanted to help Kady through it.

"Maybe I could slip away during the masquerade ball," Kady said thoughtfully.

"Or don't even go to it," Austin said.

"No, Mama would certainly notice if I weren't there. She's done nothing but think about this costume and the mask and all."

Austin felt the gleam of an idea. "That's it—the mask!"

"What do you mean?" Charlotte said.

"What if someone else came in the costume and mask and wig? Aunt Olivia would think it was you, and she'd never even suspect you were gone."

Kady's eyes lit up a little. "I wish you were bigger, Charlotte. You would be a perfect stand-in."

Austin gnawed his lip for a second. "What about Polly?"

They both stared at him.

"No," Charlotte said at once. "She'd tell Mama in a minute!"

"I don't know," Kady said. "She's been a lot more trustworthy lately. Do you really think she'd do it, Austin?" And then before he could answer, she shook her head. "No, I can't take a chance. This is the whole rest of my life we're talking about here."

There was a rap on the door. Polly didn't wait for them to invite her in before she pushed it open and stuck her thin-curled head inside.

"Mama is looking all over for you," she said. Her birdlike eyes narrowed suspiciously. "What's going on in here? Are you three up to something?"

Austin tried to look innocent, but he knew if he looked anything like Charlotte did, he was failing miserably. Only Kady seemed to be able to conceal the turmoil that was bubbling under her surface.

"We were just talking about you," she said.

"I'm sure you were," Polly said, her face tightening. "It doesn't seem to matter what I do, you all still treat me like an outsider."

"No, it was nothing like that," Kady said. Austin felt her nudge his leg slightly. "We were just saying how you were the perfect person to help us out with something."

Polly still looked doubtful, but she crossed her arms over her chest and moved closer to them. "How?" she said. "With what?"

Charlotte looked like she was going to faint. But Austin felt a tingle. He couldn't wait to see how Kady was going to pull *this* one off.

"I don't want to go to the ball tonight," Kady said.

"You're such an old stick-in-the-mud, Kady," Polly said. "I'd trade places with you in a minute."

"Then will you?"

Polly looked as if she were trying not to throw herself into Kady's arms. "Do you mean, wear your costume and your wig and everything? Pretend I'm you?"

"Precisely," Kady said. "Then we could both have what we wanted."

Polly's face broke into a smile. That didn't happen often. Whenever it did, Austin always thought she looked so much better without that thin scowl on her face. But just as quickly, the smile disappeared, and Polly squinted at each of them in turn.

"This is not just about you not wanting to go to the party, Kady," she said. "You three look too serious for that. What are you going to do *instead* of coming to the ball?"

"Nothing you'd be interested in, really," Kady said.

"There you go," Polly said, her voice going up an octave. "Leaving me out, acting like I don't have any feelings or thoughts like the rest of you!"

"We think you have thoughts and feelings!" Austin said. "It's just—"

He looked helplessly at the girls. It was Charlotte, surprisingly, who opened her mouth.

"We just don't want you to have to lie to Mama," she said. "We know how close you are to her."

Polly pinched in her forehead. "I'm not close to her right now. She's being completely unreasonable about this party. You can tell me anything. I won't breathe a word to her."

"Really, Polly—" Kady began.

"No." Polly jerked her head. "If you don't tell me the truth, I won't help you. I'm as much a part of this family as anybody else."

Austin wasn't sure, but he thought he caught a hint of tears making her voice quaver. He couldn't really blame her. He remembered what it was like to feel like a misfit, when he'd first come to South Carolina. Besides, no more tears. He was getting really tired of tears.

"I think you can tell her, Kady," he said.

Kady thought about it for a minute, and then she sighed.

"I'm going out to meet a beau," she said. "It's someone I love very much—the first one ever, in fact."

"Oh!" Polly said.

Austin watched in amazement as her face transformed from the pouting younger sister to a fairy godmother. Her eyes softened and her cheeks grew pink and she smiled as if her own dreams were coming true.

"How romantic, Kady!" she said. "I'm so happy for you! What's his name?"

"I don't have time to go into all of that now," Kady said. She looked a little shocked. "I'll tell you all about it later, I promise."

"I want every detail," Polly said. She actually clapped her little claw hands. "This is exciting. Come on, let's go upstairs so I can try on the dress."

She grabbed Kady by the arm and dragged her to the door, chattering like a chipmunk.

"It's a good thing Mama arranged for a wig and a mask," she said. "She'll never suspect a thing. I think I can even talk like you. . . ."

When the door closed behind them, Charlotte looked at Austin with a surprised smile. "Well," she said, "that was easy!"

But as it turned out, that wasn't the end of it.

By the afternoon, Aunt Olivia was in a frenzy. She stationed Austin, Charlotte, and Jefferson outside to intercept all delivery people and point them in the right direction.

"Flowers come in the front door, food goes to the kitchen building, and the burgundy runner for the stairs comes in the side door," she told them.

"Burgundy runner for the stairs?" Austin said to Charlotte. "What's that for?"

"To protect the carpets," she said. "Mama thinks of everything."

They had just started a game of sheepmeat on the sidewalk, in which they tossed a ball of yarn back and forth as they ran, when a slave boy in bare feet hurried up to the gate.

"He's bringing something for the party," Austin said. "We're supposed to catch him before he goes inside."

"I don't think so," Charlotte said. "He isn't wearing a livery uniform. He's come from the poor section."

But Austin went up to him anyway, stopping him before he could open the gate.

"What do you have?" Austin said.

The boy looked nervously at his paper-wrapped package. "Just a ham for Miz Ravenal," he said.

"That goes in the kitchen building," Austin said. "I'll take you there."

He led the way through the gate, looking triumphantly at Charlotte. But she handed the yarn to Jefferson, told him to wait there, and hurried after Austin.

"Mama isn't serving ham at the party," she whispered to Austin. "They're having quail, remember?"

Austin cocked his head at her. "Maybe it's for tomorrow. . . ."

But even as he said it, his voice trailed off. This was the second ham that had been delivered to the townhouse in a few days. And he didn't remember having any ham at all at the table.

"I'll take that from you," Austin said to the slave. "I'll see that it gets to Miz Ravenal."

"Miz Kady Ravenal," the boy said. And then with his eyes lowered, he dashed off.

Austin and Charlotte only stared at each other for a moment before they, too, tore off—to find Kady.

She was in her room brushing her hair and looking bright-eyed, as if she couldn't wait for evening. Her eyes grew somber when she took the package they handed her.

"You are so smart," she said. "This could have been a disaster if anyone else had gotten hold of it."

"What is it?" Austin said.

Kady quickly checked the hall to be sure no one was lurking about before she unwrapped the paper from the ham and examined it carefully. There was some tiny writing on the inside of the paper. When she'd read it, she said, "Oh, no!"

"What's wrong?" Charlotte said.

"Bad ham?" Austin said.

"No! I have to get word to a maroon at the edge of town that he must be . . . well, he must be at a certain place at a certain time to be smuggled on to freedom."

"What's a maroon?" Austin said.

"A fugitive slave in hiding."

"Don't you always do that?" Austin said.

"Yes, but this is at the very same time I'm to meet Fitz! I can't do both!"

It was the first time Austin had ever seen Kady look hopeless. Her big eyes misted, and she began to pace. Charlotte looked like she wanted to cry, too. There was almost no one in the world she loved more than Kady.

Tears again? Austin thought. *Can we do nothing but cry here?*

To keep him*self* from bawling, he thought hard.

"Does it have to be tonight?" he said. "Can't it wait until tomorrow?"

"No. Saturday is the best day to escape. The newspapers won't print ads on Sunday, so it gives the slave a head start. This one is going to need it. He walks all stoop-shouldered from being beaten." Kady went restlessly to the window. "And it's going to be a clear night. He'll be able to see the North Star perfectly. That's how he'll know which way to go."

"What do you have to do to get the word to the slave?" Austin said.

"Deliver this ham. There's a message for him in the bone. He'll know that."

"Then why can't we deliver it—Charlotte and me?"

Kady stopped, but she shook her head.

"Too dangerous," she said.

"Why? You were going to do it."

"You would have to drive the wagon all the way to Venning's Wharf—it's the last one to the north."

"Is it rough there?" Austin said. "Are there thieves and murderers?"

"No, of course not. But—"

"Then let us go," Charlotte said. "We want to help you."

"This could be your last chance to marry Fitz," Austin said. He felt a little sly. "And you can never tell how long Polly is going to be able to keep a secret."

Kady sank down onto her bed. "All right," she said. "But you have to do everything just as I say."

They listened with rapt attention. Kady repeated everything three times and made them repeat it back to her. By dusk, when Polly was practically beating down the door, eager to slip into Kady's costume, they were ready.

But right away, they ran into an obstacle. They were hurrying toward White Point Garden to find the wagon Kady said would be there, hitched to a horse, when a voice hailed them from behind.

"Jus' a minute now!" Henry-James called out. "Where you think you goin'?"

Austin's heart sank. Beside him, Charlotte stopped and waited for Henry-James to catch up.

"We're going for a ride," she said innocently.

"Not without me, you ain't. Marse Drayton, he done tol' me—"

"I know," Charlotte said. "But you can't go where we're going. You'll get in trouble if they catch you without a pass."

"Marse Drayton, he always give me a pass when I takes you chilrun out," he said. "I'll go get one."

Charlotte couldn't answer that one. Austin studied the toe of his shoe.

"He don't know you's goin' neither, does he?" Henry-James said. His big, black eyes went into slits as he stared at Austin. "What you up to, Massa Austin?"

"We're just doing an errand for Kady," Austin said. "I promise you, we'll be right back."

"What you gonna do if'n them Fire Eaters sees you? They'd snatch you up so fast—"

"How can they see me?" Austin said. "It's night!"

"And besides," Charlotte put in, "they're all going to be at Mama's masquerade ball. She's invited everyone so Daddy will have a chance to try to soften them up and change their minds."

"You sure?" Henry-James said.

"Positive," Charlotte said. She patted Henry-James's arm. "We'll be all right."

"And if we don't come back by ten o'clock, you can come looking for us," Austin said. "We're going to Venning's Wharf."

"Way up north?" Henry-James said.

Charlotte answered by tugging on Austin's arm. "We'll be fine," she said. "Bye!"

It wasn't until they had tucked the ham under the blanket in the back and climbed up into the wagon that Austin said, "Do you know how to drive?"

"Of course," Charlotte said. "Isaac taught me, and sometimes Seton used to let me drive. Do you remember him?"

Austin did. Seton was a big, kind man who had been Uncle Drayton's body slave before Henry-James. He'd run away soon after Austin had arrived. The thought of him, now free somewhere, made Austin puff up his chest.

"I'm glad we're doing this," he said as Charlotte gently guided the horse out of the park and onto the South Battery. "I like helping the slaves get away."

"There are so many of them, though," Charlotte said. "How much difference can just one make?"

"You heard what Kady said this afternoon," Austin said. "One is better than none. You just have to do it one at a time. I heard tell that Harriet Tubman has helped 300 slaves get away."

"Is she the lady whose picture is on all those wanted posters?"

Austin nodded. "They call her 'Moses.' "

Charlotte's eyes widened. "There's a $40,000 reward for her capture!"

"Huh," Austin said. "Then you know what I'm gonna do?"

"What?"

"Every time I see one of those posters, I'm gonna tear it down."

Charlotte nodded her head with satisfaction and clicked her tongue at the horse to move faster. The cold air rushing past them made Austin shrink into his jacket.

"What a miserable time to be running away," he said.

"I know," Charlotte said, "but remember, Kady told us it was better for them to go in winter. The ground's hard so they don't leave tracks, and the rivers north of here will be frozen so they can walk across them."

"Besides," Austin said, watching yet another carriage pass

them on its way to the Ravenals', "everybody is so busy with parties, they're not paying as much attention."

Charlotte grinned. "I think this is going to be easy, Boston," she said. "Kady's going to be so proud."

Austin thought so, too.

Until a cart flew out from an alley and stopped right in front of them. The wagon's horse reared up and shuffled to a stop, and Charlotte leaned back, pulling on the reins and shaking.

A large-chested man in a soldier's hat emerged from the cart and stalked toward them, shouting, "Halt now! Who goes there?"

✢ ⟡ ✢

Chapter Eleven

"Let me do the talking," Austin whispered to Charlotte as the man approached.

Charlotte didn't look as if she could have uttered a word anyway. Her face was ashen as she hopped down from the wagon beside Austin. He led her away from it to meet the soldier—away from the wagon and the ham.

The soldier stopped them and put his hands on his hips. His chest seemed to expand to the size of a barrel. Austin swallowed hard.

"What are you children doin' out and about in the dark?" he said.

Kady said if we get stopped to tell as much truth as we can, Austin thought.

"We're going on an errand," he said.

"What kind of errand?"

"We're just taking something to a friend," Austin said. "He's staying north of here. Everybody is so busy at our house—what with the parties and everything—that they sent us. We just get underfoot at times like this. You know how children are."

The soldier looked as if he did—and as if he didn't care much for "underfoot" children. His eyes flickered over to Charlotte.

"Well, now," he said. "If I were your daddy, I wouldn't be sending a pretty little thing like you out on a night errand, that's for sure."

Austin took a second to look at Charlotte. She was just about his best friend. But he'd never thought of her as a "pretty little thing."

Charlotte had never thought of herself that way either, that was obvious. She stared blankly at the soldier and then began to roll up the apron on her dress, the way she always did when she was uncertain.

"May we be on our way now, sir?" Austin said brightly. "We really do have to get these things to—"

"Not before I see what 'these things' are," the soldier said. He expanded his big chest even further and stepped around them. "I have my orders. I'm to search all suspicious-looking vehicles that pass this way. We can't be too careful, not since the secession. There are enemies everywhere."

"This is a suspicious-looking vehicle?" Austin said, hurrying after the soldier. Behind him he could feel Charlotte freezing in her tracks. His own heart was slamming against his chest.

"It is when it's driven by two children, and one of them no more than a little doll."

Austin tried to keep his voice cheerful, even while his throat wanted to scream for help. "We aren't exactly children," he said. "I'm just a week short of 12 myself."

"And your pretty sister?" the soldier said, hiking himself up to the side of the wagon.

"She's the same age," Austin said without thinking.

"You're twins, then?" the soldier said. "Huh. She's a lot prettier than you, boy."

Austin tried to laugh. "I don't think I want to be pretty anyway," he said. But his head was shouting, *He's going to find the ham! He's going to tear it open! He's going to know!*

The soldier did none of those things. He turned from the wagon and glowered at Austin.

"Why did you lie to me, boy?" he said.

"Lie?" Austin said. Which lie was he talking about?

"Why did you tell me you were delivering something when there isn't a thing in this here wagon?"

Austin couldn't help it. He leaped up onto the wagon wheel and peered inside. The soldier was right. It was empty. There wasn't a ham in sight.

Austin's mind raced. "What happened to all our things?" he said. "Someone's stolen them all!"

He looked around desperately for Charlotte. She was staring at him, eyes about to spring from her face. Even in the dim evening light he could see that her freckles were standing out.

"I ought to haul both of you in to my colonel," the soldier said gruffly. "Something ain't right here."

"That's for sure," Austin said. "We've been robbed!"

"Huh," the soldier said.

He shook his head at Austin and shifted his eyes to Charlotte.

"I'm sorry, pretty little thing," he said. "You shouldn't let your ornery brother drag you into messes like this. Make him take you on home now, 'fore somethin' bad happens to you."

Charlotte managed to nod.

The soldier gave Austin one more glaring look before he stomped off to his cart and scooted it on down Calhoun Street. He was well out of sight before Austin sagged against the wagon. Charlotte fluttered to him like a baby bird.

"What happened to the ham?" she whispered. "Where did it go?"

"Right here," a voice hissed up to them.

Austin ducked his head to look under the wagon. Tucked behind the wheel was Henry-James.

"What on earth?" Austin said.

Henry-James crawled out and presented him with the ham, still wrapped safely in its paper.

"You didn't think I was gonna let you two chilrun do this fool thing on your own, did you?" he said. "I'd sooner cut off my own head."

"We almost got ours cut off!" Austin said. "How did you get that ham out of there without him seeing you?"

"I was in the blame wagon the whole time," Henry-James said with disgust. "If'n you two is gonna smuggle slaves, you gon' have to be more aware of your surroundin's." He shook his head. "I got in while you was busy discussin' whether Miz Lottie knowed how to drive."

"And you just slithered out while we were talking to the soldier?" Charlotte said.

Henry-James gave a grin that revealed the gap between his two front teeth. "While he was goin' on 'bout how purty you is, Miz Lottie."

"He's a liar," Charlotte said. She flounced her hair over her shoulders a little too hard. "I'm not pretty. Mama would be the first one to tell you so."

I don't believe much of what Aunt Olivia says, Austin thought. He looked closely at Charlotte. *I guess she's pretty. But who cares? She's just . . . Charlotte.*

"If'n you gonna get this here ham where it s'pose to go," Henry-James said, "we gots to get goin'."

Austin shook Charlotte-thoughts out of his head and climbed back up into the wagon. Henry-James dove under the blanket, where they seemed to be spending a good deal of their time lately, and Charlotte took the reins.

They got to Venning's Wharf without further mishap. Austin was glad of that. As nervous as they were now, any one of them would have fainted dead away at the sight of another soldier.

Just as Kady had told them, Venning's was at the

northernmost edge of Charleston. There were few buildings there, or trees either, so the wind off the river was harsh and bone-chilling. Austin liked it. It gave him an excuse to let his teeth chatter.

Henry-James stayed out of sight under the blanket, though he assured them he would be watching their every move and would be right there if they had any more trouble.

Austin let Charlotte carry the ham, which seemed like something a girl would do, and he walked briskly along to the boathouse Kady had directed them to, acting as if he knew exactly what he was doing. Kady had directed him to do that, too. He knocked on the door like she'd told him—three hard knocks and three little quick ones.

From inside, a shaky voice said, "Who's there?"

"A friend with friends," Austin said.

Kady had told them that was the secret code. He'd thought he'd be thrilled to use it. Right now, though, he was aching with fear.

"What do you have?" came the expected answer.

"I've been sent with one medium ham," Austin answered.

They waited, breath held, until the door slowly came open a crack. A black face peeked out from a yoke of stooped shoulders.

"Here's your ham," Austin whispered to him. "Jesus will be with you."

The black head nodded. A hand came out and took the ham from Charlotte, pulled it inside, and closed the door. Charlotte took Austin's sleeve and hung on as they walked quickly back to the wagon and swung on board.

"Everything all right, Miz Lottie?" Henry-James whispered to them.

"It's all right," Charlotte said. "He'll be off to freedom tomorrow."

"He's one lucky boy, then," Henry-James said.

His voice was quiet, wistful. It sent a pang through Austin that he didn't recognize.

"Did Kady tell you to say that last part about Jesus?" Charlotte said as they headed back to the city. "I don't remember that."

"No," Austin said. "It just came out of my mouth."

"I hope you're right," Charlotte said. "I know how I would feel if somebody I loved—like Henry-James—was running away. I'd want Jesus to be with him."

Austin shivered as she drove on. It wasn't from the cold. It was from the thought that shuddered across his mind. The sound of Henry-James's voice just now. The secret between him and Kady. What Charlotte had just said.

Is Henry-James thinking of running away? he thought.

Austin had been in some dangerous situations in the past few days, constantly hiding under blankets and sneaking in and out of shadows. But none of that was as frightening as that last thought. It was so cold, so dark, so fearful a thought that he couldn't stand to have it in his head.

Jesus, please, no, he prayed. *Don't let Henry-James do that. Please don't let him try to run.*

He was glad to see the candlelight and the lamps still burning in the Ravenal townhouse when they'd left the wagon at the park and crept inside the gate. Anything to take his mind off what he'd just thought.

"Let's peek in through the window," Charlotte said, pulling both boys behind a row of camellia bushes smothered with their winter flowers. "I want to see how Polly is doing."

"Miz Polly?" Henry-James said. "She ain't at the party. We ain't heard nothin' *but* her caterwaulin' 'bout that ever since we been here."

Austin poked Charlotte, and she clamped her mouth shut. They squatted down under the window of the ballroom and slowly rose until their eyes were just above the sill. Inside, dancers in glittering costumes were swirling past, laughing into each other's masked faces as they danced by. Austin caught sight of Aunt Olivia in her Spanish lady costume doing the two-step with tall, gangly Virgil Rhett, and he saw Uncle Drayton, dressed as a bullfighter, talking in the corner with Chesnut and Pryor. It all reminded him of a confusing dream.

"There's Miz Kady!" Henry-James said. "Right there, just a-dancin' with that there count."

"He's just *dressed* like a count," Charlotte said.

Henry-James was right. Decked from head to toe like Queen Elizabeth, Polly was the image of Kady.

"Don't she look purty?" Henry-James said. "She look like she havin' the time o' her life. I hopes Marse Fitzgerald don't mind."

Austin didn't dare look at Charlotte. He knew he wouldn't be able to keep from laughing.

Maybe everything really was going to be all right. Maybe if Father sent for them now, Austin could go and feel as if he were finished here. He'd be sad—but he'd be finished. Was this what it meant to *feel* that what you were doing was right?

It was long past midnight when the ball ended. Austin was still awake, waiting to hear Polly pass on her way to her room, hoping that Aunt Olivia wouldn't want to go to Kady and find out if she had indeed been swept off her feet.

But he fell asleep before he ever heard Aunt Olivia come upstairs, and when he awoke the next morning, there were no shrieks from below, the way there would have been if Kady's absence had been discovered.

I wonder what that's going to be like, Austin thought as he lay in bed watching the sun try to get through the crack between the shutters. *Are they going to go out searching for her? Will they send the police to try and find her? And when she does come home, what will they say about Fitz?*

He didn't really want to think about that. He'd decided to get up and get busy with something else when he heard the bell at the front door ring. An anxious feeling crept into his chest. Was that Kady now, bringing home her new husband?

His mother stirred in her bed, and Jefferson's curly head popped up from his cot.

"Who is that at the door so early?" Mother said. "It is impossible to get any sleep around here. A war itself couldn't be noisier!"

Austin heard footsteps hurrying to answer the door as he whipped off his nightshirt and wriggled into a pair of woolen knickers and a cotton shirt. Something unusual was happening, and he wanted to be ready for it.

But before he could pull on his stockings, someone was hurrying up the stairs and knocking on doors.

"Wake up, Miz Polly!" Mousie was saying. "Miz Charlotte! Miz Kady!"

Austin stopped, his stocking pulled only partway over his toes, and listened. But Mousie moved right on, tapping at their door next.

"Miz Sally," Mousie's high little voice said, "Marse Drayton say come on downstairs."

Mother's eyes grew unsettled, and she pulled on her dressing gown.

"Come on, boys," she said. "This doesn't sound good."

Austin's chest sizzled, and he tried to think of what he was going to say when Uncle Drayton asked if they'd had anything to do with Kady's strange disappearance. They had before—it was only logical that he should ask.

I'll tell the truth, Austin thought. *I did what I thought was right. I was just going through the narrow gate, the way Daddy Elias said.*

He wanted to tell Charlotte that, but she was already downstairs when he got there, wedged between her mother and Polly on the sofa in the drawing room. Uncle Drayton's face was drawn as he watched the Hutchinsons come in and get settled.

"What is it, Drayton?" Aunt Olivia said. "Forevermore, I cannot stand this suspense."

"I just thought it was only right to gather you all together to tell you this," Uncle Drayton said. "I know he's just a slave, but he's been with us for so long. Even Sally remembers—"

"Who?" Aunt Olivia said. "Drayton, please!"

But suddenly Austin already knew. He could have said Uncle Drayton's words with him.

"I'm sorry, my dears," Uncle Drayton said. "Daddy Elias is dying."

✠ ✠ ✠

Chapter Twelve

*I*t didn't feel real to Austin. How could Josephine still be hauling the water in from the well and Tot still be carrying a chamber pot down from the bedroom and Mousie still be tipping the pie crust table up in front of the fireplace so Aunt Olivia's wax makeup wouldn't run—how could all that still be going on just as usual if Daddy Elias were dying?

Shouldn't the world be stopping for him?

But it went on. Uncle Drayton looked in the corner at Henry-James, who hadn't moved since his master had made the announcement.

"We'll go back to Canaan Grove," he said, "so you can see to things."

"How long will you be gone, Drayton?" Aunt Olivia said. "There's the reception at the Rhetts' tonight—"

"As long as it takes, Olivia," Uncle Drayton said, his voice stretched tight.

Aunt Olivia pressed her lips together and was still, except for the telltale quivering chins.

"There will be a funeral to arrange, and I'll need to put a new overseer in charge," he continued. "It's a good thing we're still a month away from planting."

Austin thought he would explode. *How can you think about planting when Daddy Elias needs us?* he wanted to shout at his uncle. *We have to go back and save him!*

But it was Charlotte who spoke, and none too softly.

"I'm going with you, Daddy," she said.

"Now, Charlotte," Aunt Olivia opened her pressed-in lips to say, "I'm having the ladies in for tea tomorrow. I told you I wanted you there. You can wear that new dress you got for Christmas—"

"I don't care about that old dress!" Charlotte cried. "I want to be with Henry-James! I want to say good-bye to Daddy Elias!"

Aunt Olivia gave an exaggerated gasp, as if Charlotte had struck her across the face. She recovered quickly, though, and her eyes smoldered like a pair of coals.

"You are getting to be just like Kady," Aunt Olivia said. "I should never have let her give you your lessons—I should have sent you to Miss Orlis's School a year ago, when there was still hope. . . ." Her voice trailed off, and she looked around. "Where is Kady, anyway?"

Austin felt his hands go cold. He fumbled for something to say, but Polly beat him to it.

"She's probably still sleeping," she said. "She had quite a full evening, I understand." She patted her mother's leg. "I'll tell her the news when she wakes up. Let's not spoil her wonderful night, shall we?"

The room itself seemed to stare at Polly in disbelief.

I guess you really do learn who your friends are when it gets down to the important things, Austin thought. For a brief second, it took the sting out of Austin's chest. When it came back, he said, "Uncle Drayton, I want to go back to Canaan Grove, too—please."

"Well, good heavens, then go—all of you," Aunt Olivia said. "I'll stay here and try to hold this family's name together!"

"Do that, would you, Olivia?" Uncle Drayton said. His voice sounded weary, and he looked as if one more argument would crack his shoulders in two. "Get ready, Charlotte, Austin. Jefferson, little man, I'm sure you'll want to come along."

Jefferson, for once, hadn't said a word. He nodded his tousled head and then sank fearfully against his mother. Austin wanted to do the same thing. The world was suddenly more frightening than he'd ever known it to be. Daddy Elias was dying.

We just won't let him, Austin thought. *We'll get there in time, and he won't die.*

Within an hour they were aboard the packet boat, steaming back up the Ashley River toward the plantation. It was gray-cold and drizzling, but Austin and Charlotte decided to ride up on the deck with Henry-James. They didn't say much as they watched the brackish water churn past them. It was just good, as if standing side by side let them know they would still be together tomorrow. For suddenly, tomorrow didn't look so certain anymore.

They were damp and chilled to the bone when they arrived, but no one stopped to change or dry out in the Big House. Henry-James led the way straight to the cabin on Slave Street. Austin found himself holding his breath until he heard Ria's soft singing from behind the shutters.

Massa sleeps in the feather bed,
Black man sleeps on the floor;
When we get to heaven
There'll be no slaves no more.

She wouldn't be doing that, Austin knew, if Daddy Elias were already gone.

The cabin was smoky from the fireplace and the tallow candles Ria had burning, but it was as warm and as cozy as it had always been. Daddy Elias even looked up from the straw-and-rags bed on the floor in front of the fire and gave them his spoon-shaped smile. It was the size of a teaspoon, but it was there. Austin hurried to him, nearly tripping over Bogie, who was stretched out at the old man's side.

Bogie moaned low in his throat and dug his floppy face into Henry-James's lap when he, too, knelt down next to his grandfather. Austin could feel Charlotte and Jefferson on either side of him. Uncle Drayton came to stand with them. The circle they formed seemed to quiet the rattle in Daddy Elias's chest.

I knew we could save him, Austin thought. But even as he thought it, it seemed silly. Although his old friend was smiling, some of the light had faded from his eyes. He seemed to be looking at them from someplace far away.

"How are you doing, Old Daddy?" Uncle Drayton said from above them.

"Marse Drayton?" Daddy Elias said. His breath caught and for an awful second, Austin thought it had stopped. "Is that you, Marse?" he said.

"It is. What can I do for you?"

"You just tell me I done been a good servant to you, Marse Drayton," Daddy Elias said. His voice was so faint and crackled that it was hard to hear it, but Uncle Drayton obviously did. He squatted down by Daddy Elias's head and with an almost imperceptible touch put his hand on the old man's gray hair.

"You're the best Canaan Grove has ever seen," Uncle Drayton said. "It wouldn't be what it is without you."

Austin took his eyes away from Daddy Elias long enough to look at his uncle. He seemed sad and tender, and in that instant Austin knew what he must have looked like when he was young like Charlotte and himself. He had probably come to this cabin, too, and listened to Daddy Elias's stories. It looked as if Uncle Drayton had loved him just like they did.

"That's all I needs to hear," Daddy Elias said. "Now I can go to Jesus in peace."

"Not until I ask you something," Uncle Drayton said.

Austin felt Ria stir at her place on the other side of her father. "He plenty tired, Marse Drayton," she said.

"Then I'll be quick," he said. "Have I ever mistreated you, Daddy Elias?"

Daddy Elias closed his eyes. "Anything you done wrong, I done forgive you for that long ago. And the Lord Jesus, I know He done, too."

"Then that's all *I* needed to hear," Uncle Drayton said. He closed his eyes for a second and nodded and then he straightened up. "I'll leave you all in peace. Children, don't you stay too long."

He went quietly to the door, Bogie tapping his toenails across the floor as he saw him out.

"He done been a good massa," Daddy Elias mumbled. "He ain't never sold none of us away from each other."

Ria cleared her throat. "I thank *God* for that," she said. She didn't add "not Marse Drayton," but Austin could hear it in her voice.

How can Daddy Elias forgive somebody who's kept him a slave all his life and lets him die on a bunch of dirty rags on the floor? How can he do that, God?

Austin didn't even realize he was praying. But he got an answer right away.

"I been proud to be a servant," Daddy Elias said in his fading voice. "Marse Jesus, He come to us as a servant—we all gots to remember that. He done suffered more than we have."

"You *have* suffered," Austin said.

But Daddy Elias shook his head. "No, Massa Austin. Marse Jesus, He done give me joy, and that done carried me right up above them frosted feet and that ol' burnin' sun and this here ol' damp cabin. He done give me hope. Now I'm gonna get me my reward."

What reward? Austin thought.

He looked at Charlotte, but she was crying without a sound. Henry-James had his face buried in Bogie's neck. Ria was holding her face still. There was no one to ask but Daddy Elias himself.

"What reward, Daddy Elias?" Austin said.

"I done obeyed Marse Drayton, and Marse Henry 'fore him," he said. "But I obeyed Marse Jesus before anybody—and He gonna reward me for that once I gets to heaven. And I's comin' now, Lord."

Austin wanted to shake his head and scream out, "No! Ria, do something!"

But he couldn't disturb the peace on Daddy Elias's face.

The spoon-shaped smile suddenly sprang to his lips, as bright and clear as the first time Austin had met him.

"Henry-James," the old man said, "did you hear what Marse Drayton said 'bout me helpin' make Canaan Grove?"

"Yessir," Henry-James said. His voice was flat, as if he weren't feeling anything at all.

"You remember that, boy," he said. "You get that good feelin' in you, too."

Austin was confused. He wanted to ask Daddy Elias about that—about whether Henry-James should just be content to be a slave and obey everything Uncle Drayton said, even when it was wrong. But it hit him like a board in the face—there wasn't any more time for questions now. And there never would be again.

"Massa Austin," Daddy Elias said, licking his lips but not even getting them moist. "I'm glad you got to know Marse Jesus. Yessir, I sure 'nuff am."

"Me, too," Austin said.

"You remember now, no matter how narrow that ol' gate get, the Lord always gonna be there to get you through."

"I'll remember," Austin said.

The old man seemed to be looking for someone, but he closed his eyes. "Massa Jefferson, you make sure your brother tell you them Jesus stories every day now, you hear?"

Jefferson nodded, but he looked very lost.

As for Charlotte, Daddy Elias just held out his hand. She took it and squeezed it.

And then they left, all but Henry-James and Ria, and sat on

the front stoop of the little cabin where they'd sat so many times listening to Daddy Elias's stories and hearing Ria humming inside while she cooked. Daddy Elias had always tapped his toe to her tunes.

Jefferson shivered and crept close to Austin. He put his arm around his little brother and held on. Charlotte moved closer, too. They sat huddled like a miserable trio of drenched puppies.

"Everything looks so empty," Charlotte said.

"I never knew anybody who died before," Jefferson said. "It's scaring me."

Charlotte looked over his head at Austin. "Do you think people ever feel happy again after somebody dies?"

The question chilled Austin, and for once he didn't have an answer. He could only think of one thing.

"Daddy Elias didn't look sad," he said. "He was smiling."

"Why?" Jefferson said. "Why isn't he scared?"

"I guess it's because he knows he's going to see Jesus," Austin said.

They were all quiet then, and Austin thought deep in his head.

Am I going to feel like that when I die? he thought. *Am I gonna know I'm a person Jesus is going to welcome into heaven, like Daddy Elias knows?*

His chest burned with the worst anxiety yet. *What if I'm not? But I try so hard! I pray—and I still don't know what to do sometimes. What am I going to do without Daddy Elias to tell me?*

From inside the cabin, there was a low singing sound. At first Austin thought it was Ria, and he let out a breath. She was still singing. It was still all right.

But the singing sound grew louder and more mournful. And Austin knew it wasn't Ria.

It was Bogie, announcing that dear old Daddy Elias had gone to his reward.

They held the funeral the next day in the late afternoon, after the slaves had had a chance to bathe Daddy Elias and dress him in his black Sunday suit. He looked dignified and peaceful to Austin as he lay in the coffin the slaves had made out of old boards blackened with shoe polish down in the carpentry shop. He looked just the way he did when he was sitting up in the balcony in church, listening to Reverend Pullens preach his sermons.

"I never saw a dead person before," Jefferson said as he stared into the coffin. "Why doesn't he look dead?"

"Because he's livin' with Jesus now," Ria told him.

At least I was right about one thing, Austin thought. He tried not to let it scare him.

That morning, Uncle Drayton had told Ria he was giving Daddy Elias a proper funeral.

"Why wouldn't he?" Austin whispered to Charlotte.

"Most times, a slave gets buried at night after work," she said. "He gives them a few hours off to do it so it won't interrupt the planting and things."

For Daddy Elias, however, Uncle Drayton saw to it that the praying and the Bible reading were done in the big elegant back hallway of the Big House. All the slaves who wouldn't fit inside gathered on the porch and listened while they prayed and heard the Bible read and sang all of Daddy Elias's old favorites—"Swing Low, Sweet Chariot," "Crossing Over Jordan," and "Bound for the Promised Land."

The same little girls who had sung like angels at Christmas gathered at the back door and sang a song that would have brought the spoon-smile to Daddy Elias's face.

I want to be an angel, and with an angel stand,
A crown upon my forehead, a harp within my hand.
Right there before my Savior, so glorious and so bright,
I'll hear the sweetest music, and praise Him day and night.

Uncle Drayton said a few words before they carried the coffin out.

"Elias was a true servant of Christ," he said. "He performed his service cheerfully, and not just when his master was watching."

"Amen," the slaves all said.

Most of them wailed and cried out loud as they lit their pine knots from a torch Isaac held up and followed the black hearse drawn by two black horses that carried Daddy Elias's body to the slaves' graveyard.

It was sunset by then, and Ria gave a faint smile.

"He always loved the sunset, Daddy 'Lias did," she said. "That mean it were the end of the workin' day. And now all his trials and work be over."

There was one spreading magnolia in the cemetery, and Daddy Elias's grave was ready just beneath it. Charlotte saw the hole in the ground and started to sob with the slaves. Austin held tight to Jefferson's hand and tried not to be afraid.

"He's not really going down there," he whispered to his little brother—as much for himself as for Jefferson. "Remember, he's already gone to live with Jesus."

As Isaac and some of the other strong slaves covered the coffin with dirt, the women slaves circled the grave, singing and dancing.

Going to carry this body
To the graveyard,
Graveyard, don't you know me?
To lay this body down.

Ria put the last article Daddy Elias had used before he died—his old chipped cup—nearby, and the slave children decorated the top of the grave with broken bits of pottery and colored glass. And then they all looked at Henry-James.

"You the man of our family now, Henry-James," his mother said. "You got to send Daddy 'Lias off now and take your place."

Austin felt the biggest lump yet growing in his throat. How could Henry-James do that, when his eyes were all swollen from crying and his lips were trembling so?

But Henry-James stepped forward and bowed his head, and all the slaves did the same.

"Lord," he said, "we givin' You our Daddy 'Lias. He done us good. He shown us You. You gets to keep him now, while we carries on. Help us do that, Marse Jesus."

That was all he could say. But it was enough. And suddenly the air was alive with more singing—joyful songs this time, with clapping and more dancing.

"Why is everybody so happy?" Jefferson said. His blue eyes were cloudy and confused.

" 'Cause Daddy Elias happy now," Ria said. "We gots to celebrate that."

Jefferson looked relieved not to have to cry anymore, and his face was suddenly wreathed with dimples. He dashed off to dance among the slave children.

But Charlotte stayed close beside Austin and gave a sigh that still shivered with her day of crying.

"I don't know how they can dance," she said. "I still feel awful."

"Me, too," Austin said.

They started out of the cemetery to go to the Big House, where the tables on the porch were groaning with collards, peas, cornbread, rice, and all of Daddy Elias's other favorites. But a voice behind them stopped them. It was still wailing, louder and more sadly than anyone that day.

They turned and saw—it was Bogie. He stopped to sniff around the grave, digging at it with his paw. Then he stopped and threw his big, baggy head back and howled.

Bogie, it seemed, felt awful, too.

✝ ⚬✝⚬ ✝

Chapter Thirteen

They left for Charleston again the next morning, and Austin was glad. Maybe if they got away from Canaan Grove, he'd be able to get rid of the fear that kept pressing on his chest.

They took Ria with them this time. Bogie wasn't happy when he watched them all board the boat, but one of the stable yard slaves promised to look after him. Still, he howled for as long as they could hear him.

Ria stayed in the boat's cabin amusing Jefferson, while Charlotte and Austin went up on the deck again with Henry-James. It was a clear, brisk day, and Austin hoped the sunshine would bring Henry-James out of the dark silence he'd kept himself in ever since the day Daddy Elias died. It was one thing to be sad, but their slave friend looked as if the whole world were ending.

On the deck, Austin found that for Henry-James, in a way it *was* ending.

"I gots somethin' to tell you two," Henry-James said finally when they had left Canaan Grove far behind. "I gots to do what Daddy 'Lias told me."

"Well, of course you do!" Austin said.

But Charlotte's face clouded. "What do you mean?" she said. "What did he tell you?"

"He done tol' me to have that good feelin' of makin' Canaan Grove what it is," he said. "He said I gots to just be the best slave I knows how and obey Marse Jesus."

Charlotte nodded solemnly. It was Austin's turn to grow stormy.

"So you're not going to read anymore and things like that?" he said. "You're just going to do every single thing Uncle Drayton tells you, even if it's wrong?"

Henry-James brought his eyebrows down in a scowl. "I guess that's what I means, Massa Austin," he said. "And that ain't all." He swallowed so hard that Austin could see his Adam's apple going up and down like it was in pain. "I can't help Miz Kady no more. And I sure wish you wouldn't do none of it either, 'cause if'n one of you gets hurt or in trouble, it gonna be my fault—and Daddy 'Lias wouldn't be proud of that!"

The last words burst out of him like they'd been trapped inside for a long time. He jerked himself away from them, went down the ladder, and disappeared into the cuddy. Austin stared after him.

"What are we going to do now?" Charlotte said.

Austin searched in his mind frantically, but he couldn't see or hear anything in there.

"I don't know, Lottie," he said. "And I hate it when I don't know."

It seemed when they got back to the townhouse in Charleston, however, that they might not have to make a decision between Henry-James and Kady after all.

"Drayton!" Aunt Olivia screeched the minute he opened the front door. "Kady Sarah is gone!"

"Gone?" he said. "What do you mean, 'gone'?"

Austin willed himself not to look at Charlotte, though she

edged closer to him and pinched his arm.

"I mean she has left this house and gone and—"

Aunt Olivia's voice cracked like a crockery plate, and she ran off to Uncle Drayton's library. But her skirt was so wide and the doorway so narrow that she bounced back and stomped her foot like a child.

Polly handed her father a piece of paper. "This will explain everything, Daddy," she said.

He wandered into the drawing room reading, followed by Aunt Olivia, Polly, Charlotte, Austin, Jefferson, and Henry-James. Austin's mother appeared soon after and came to put her arms around her sons' shoulders.

Uncle Drayton looked up with his face starchy white and his eyes just on the verge of blazing.

"I do not believe this," he said.

"What does it say?" Austin whispered to his mother.

Uncle Drayton shot him a dark look. "Let me read it to you," he said. "Let us all be perfectly clear on what Miss Kady Ravenal has done." He snapped the paper out straight and gave a hard laugh. "She writes it as a poem. She thinks this is some kind of romantic game."

Polly sighed.

She thinks it is *romantic,* Austin thought.

Uncle Drayton began to read, in a snappish voice that didn't match Kady's poetry at all:

I saw a man in the marketplace, with eyes that were gentle and kind.

I knew as I watched his tender deeds that I could love his mind.

He hasn't money, nor slaves, nor land, nor a place on the social list,

But he gives me respect and a purpose in life and all of those things I've missed.

Against the wishes I know you have for the life you want me to live
I've married this man I love so well; he has all that I have to give.
I know you'd embrace him as I do—our family he would enhance.
But because of the kind of work we must do, I cannot take that chance.
Please know that I am safe and loved and I shall want for naught;
I simply must stay in hiding now so neither of us will be caught.
The danger now is for Sally and sons, who cannot stay here long—
Get them North as soon as you can, for the South will soon do them wrong.
Farewell, my loves, I'll see you soon, if you'll smile on me again.
I cannot believe that for me to be happy, my life with you must end.

Uncle Drayton tossed the paper down on the table and stared at it as if it had ordered him to hurl himself into the harbor. Austin tried to keep his face straight, although he could hardly breathe.

"She is safe," Mother said suddenly.

"What do you know about it, Sally?" Aunt Olivia said scornfully. "You think you know everything, don't you?"

"No," Sally Hutchinson said. "But I know this."

Uncle Drayton waved off his wife with his hand and drilled his eyes into his sister. "What do you know, Sally? You are obliged to tell me."

"No, I'm obliged to keep a secret Kady entrusted to me," she said. "I just thought you should know she's safe."

"Oh, for heaven's sake!" Aunt Olivia cried. "Drayton, I will not stand for this another moment! Do as Kady says—get your sister out of here . . . and her little boys with her!"

She stormed toward the door, her skirts and Mousie bustling after her. But she stopped in the doorway, this one wide enough for her gown, and turned on Mother again.

"This is all your fault. You know that, don't you?"

"Livvy, really—"

"Don't you *Livvy* me! If it weren't for you putting all those ideas into her head, Kady would be here now entertaining decent beaus who could give her some kind of life!"

"Don't worry, Mama," Polly said. "I'll do that!"

Whether that mattered to her or not, Aunt Olivia didn't say. She flew from the room, and they heard her silky skirts rustling up the stairs.

"If you will tell me where Kady is, I can go and bring her back and put some sense into her head," Uncle Drayton said to Mother.

"I don't know where she is, Drayton."

"Then who is she with?"

"I'm not at liberty to tell you that. I only know that he will take good care of her. I know you miss her, but you have nothing to worry about—"

"Ha!" Uncle Drayton said, so loudly that the bric-a-brac on the bookshelves in the corner jiggled in their places. "That is what you told me when you ran off to marry Wesley Hutchinson. You said, 'He will take good care of me! You have nothing to worry about!' And look at you."

Mother brought herself upright on the seat beside Austin. He could feel her stiffening. "What about me?" she said.

"You are back here with *me* taking care of you. And where is your husband? Out running after some hopeless cause without a penny to his name!"

Sally Hutchinson stood up so abruptly that she nearly knocked Austin off the sofa.

"I would much rather be taken care of by that wonderful, penniless man," she said, her voice as stiff as her back, "than by the unfeeling rich man you have become! I will be gone from here just as soon as I can, Drayton—and it won't be because of Kady's warning, believe me!"

She marched from the room. Uncle Drayton took only a moment to follow her, calling, "Sally! Sally, you wait one moment!"

He'd no sooner slammed the door behind him than Charlotte put her face into her hands and began to cry.

Again, Austin thought miserably. *Is anything ever going to be the same?*

"Now, now, Miz Lottie," Henry-James said. "What you cryin' for now?"

"Everything!" Charlotte said. "Kady's gone—and Daddy will probably never let her back in the house. Daddy Elias is dead. Now Austin and Jefferson are going away for sure. I can't stand it."

Henry-James went to his knees in front of her and pried her hands away from her face. It was blotchy-red and already swelling. Austin was surprised that all these tears hadn't washed her freckles away.

"You listen to me, Miz Lottie," Henry-James said. "I's one person that ain't goin' nowhere. No matter what happen, I's gonna be right here with you, you hear me?"

Charlotte nodded.

"I's gonna be so good, Marse Drayton ain't never gonna think 'bout sellin' me again. I be here 'til the day we both dies, Miz Lottie."

That seemed to make Charlotte a little happier. She swiped the tears off her cheeks with the back of her hand and smiled when Henry-James told her to. Austin didn't feel happier at all. Something about this didn't feel right.

I can't tell when something is *right,* he thought. *But I sure can when it isn't—even when I don't know why.*

"Let's play something now," Jefferson said. "I'm sick of crying."

Henry-James and Charlotte both agreed and began to suggest games. But Austin sank back into the brocade sofa and groaned, inside and out.

What Henry-James is doing—it might make Daddy Elias happy in heaven. But what about Henry-James? What if he has to live his whole life like his grandfather lived?

Somehow, that was sadder than Daddy Elias dying.

"Come on, Austin," Charlotte said. "We're going to go play hopscotch. Henry-James, where can we get some oyster shells for that?"

"I don't want to play," Austin said. "I want to go read for a while."

He didn't really. Even though he got a book from Uncle Drayton's library—without looking at the title—he sat with it closed on his lap on the upper piazza in the sun and listened to Henry-James and Charlotte and Jefferson in the garden. Their voices were like taunts.

How can they play, he thought, *when everything is so terrible?*

He knew Daddy Elias would tell him this was the perfect time to pray to Marse Jesus for help to pass through this narrow gate.

All he could think to say was, "Please do *something*, God, because I can't do *anything*. This gate is so narrow that it's no gate at all anymore."

He opened the book and stared forlornly at the page and was about to toss it aside when he heard the clip-clop of horses' hooves in the street below. They slowed to a stop in front of the townhouse and a messenger boy jumped down from the coach and dashed toward the front door.

Austin got up and hung over the wrought-iron rail, but he could hear only snatches of the conversation at the door.

"Message for—" the messenger boy said.

"I see she gets it right off," Mousie said.

The boy dashed back to his carriage, and Austin did the same into the house and down the hall. He nearly plowed over Mousie, on her way to his mother's door.

"It's for my mother?" he said.

Mousie stuck it out at him. "You takes it to her, Massa Austin," she said in her meek little voice. "Marse Drayton in there, and they been arguin' for a hour. I's scared to death to go in there."

"I'm not scared," Austin said. And he wasn't. Everything bad that could possibly happen had already taken place.

He tapped at the door and didn't wait to be invited in. His mother and his uncle were standing in front of the window, each with their hands on their hips, faces nearly touching, eyes glittering like a pair of angry bears'.

"Austin, can this wait?" Mother said.

Austin shook his head. "You've got a message," he said.

He looked warily at his uncle. He hoped it wasn't from Kady or he'd be after her for sure.

Mother took the envelope from him and fumbled it open while Uncle Drayton paced the room, picking up Father's picture and setting it down and doing the same with the candlestick holder and the tin lamp. He stopped when she gave a startled cry.

"What is it?" Austin said. He got to her before Uncle Drayton did and peeked over her shoulder.

"It's from your father," she said. Her voice grew brittle. "He says he's on his way to get us aboard the steamship *Star of the West*." She closed her eyes. "We must be ready to slip away at a moment's notice."

✜ ✜ ✜

Chapter Fourteen

By the end of the day, the Hutchinsons had their satchels packed for a quick getaway, and once again the trunks stood ready for Uncle Drayton to send them on to ... wherever Austin and his brother and parents might end up. Every time he thought of going back to sleeping on trains and playing lonely games in the backs of lecture halls, Austin wanted to cry.

I'm getting as bad as the girls, he thought.

It seemed best to find things to do to keep himself from thinking.

"Read to us, Austin," Jefferson whined that evening when he, Austin, Charlotte, Henry-James, Polly, and Tot were all gathered in the upstairs sitting room. It was raining again, and it was as gloomy inside the house as it was outside, with Aunt Olivia constantly sniffling over Kady and Uncle Drayton brooding in his library.

"All right," Austin said. He reached for the *Charleston Mercury*, which had been left lying on the table. He cleared his throat, and the children all leaned in.

" 'Major Robert Anderson is running low on supplies at Fort Sumter'," he read. " 'It is our guess that he will not be able to hold out much longer. Once he and his troops are gone, Charleston Harbor will be free of Union military, and the South will rejoice.' "

"This is boring," Jefferson wailed.

But Austin could feel the hairs on his arms standing up. Just reading it made it seem like the war was coming right down the street toward them.

"Read something else, Austin," Polly said. "Read the ads. Those are always fun."

Austin licked his thumb and gladly turned to the advertisement section. " 'Mrs. S. A. Allen's World Hair Dressing'," he read. " 'It will remove and prevent Scurf, Dandruff, and all Unnatural Perspiration of the Head.' "

Henry-James let out a hoot, and Charlotte giggled her wonderful husky giggle.

"What's scurf?" she said.

Polly looked alarmed. "I hope I don't have it!"

Austin grinned and ran his eyes down the page. " 'Gelatin'," he read. " 'Healthy and Nutritious. No Odor and No Gluey Taste'."

"Well, I should hope not!" Polly said, clutching her chest. "I would certainly not eat anything gluey!"

"It would be hard to talk!" Charlotte said. She tried to move her lips as if they were stuck together.

Jefferson laughed so hard that he threw himself on the floor and rolled around.

"Here's another one!" Austin said. It felt good to get into the spirit of something. " 'Reward—$200!' "

"Read that, Massa Austin," said Henry-James. "I likes that one."

" 'Ran away, a NEGRO MAN named Gusta, 21 or 22 years old and stoops in his walk.' "

"Oh," Charlotte said.

Austin closed the paper, his high spirits sinking out of sight. "What about a game of Twirling the Plate?" he said.

That night, Polly and Charlotte tucked themselves in with Austin's mother, and Tot slept, snoring loudly, on the floor beside them. But even with all of them around him, breathing like the peaceful children they had a right to be, Austin lay awake with the hair standing up on his arms again and the ache growing harder in his chest.

There really was going to be a war if Major Anderson didn't leave Fort Sumter. At that very minute, he and his mother and Jefferson could have been stuck out there—

But that wasn't what bothered him most. What flashed across his mind every time he tried to close his eyes was his father. Wesley Hutchinson was coming right to Charleston on the *Star of the West*. How was he going to get to them without being caught by the Fire Eaters? Where were the answers?

If I were the kind of person Kady is—or Fitz—or Mother— I'd know.

It was so disturbing that Austin tossed until nearly dawn, going in and out of dreams about tar and feathers. Naturally, he was cranky the next day—so much so that he chose to stay home when everyone else, including his mother and Jefferson, went out coaching.

"It'll be nothing but a bunch of carriages parading through the parks and streets," he told Charlotte. "I get itchy when I ride too long."

"Then I'm staying here, too," she said. Her eyes got filmy. "We might not have many more chances to play together."

"Don't mess up this house," Aunt Olivia warned them. "You know we have the cotillion here tonight."

"What's a cotillion?" Austin said when they'd all bustled off in their jacket and skirt outfits with their enormous puffed sleeves—all except his mother, who was getting pained, double-chinned looks from Aunt Olivia for her plain cotton gown.

"It's a big dance," Charlotte said. "Lots of changing of partners and things."

"Do you know how to do it?" Austin said.

"I've watched some from the stairs."

"Show me."

Charlotte's eyes twinkled. "You want to learn how to dance, Austin? I never would have thought that."

"I want to know how to do everything," Austin said. "And besides, doing something means I don't have to think so much."

"Oh," she said, nodding knowingly. "Well, if we're going to dance, I have to have on the proper dress."

"Why?"

"Because you have to hold your skirt at just the right time." She rolled her eyes. "It's very complicated."

"Go get changed, then," he said. "I'll find a good place."

Charlotte dashed up the stairs, leaving Austin standing in the middle of the hallway thinking of the best spot for learning the cotillion, when there was a knock at the door.

At least, he thought it was a knock. It came so quietly at first that he couldn't be sure it wasn't just a bird flapping against the window.

But when it came again, he went to the door and pulled it open. There was a black woman, whose face was so hidden by the scarf she wore that Austin had to peer to make certain there really was someone inside it.

"May I help you?" he said.

Instead of answering, she pushed something at him with both hands. It was a lumpy sort of package, wrapped in paper.

"Who is this for?" Austin said.

"Miz Ravenal," she said.

"All right. I'll see she gets it when she comes home."

"Right away," the woman said. Austin saw her eyes shift nervously. "See Miz Kady get it right away."

"Oh!" Austin said. But before he could stop her, the woman had skittered like a bird down the steps and was practically flying across the yard to the gate.

Austin stopped himself from calling after her. He'd been about to tell her that Kady didn't live there anymore. But a familiar smell came up from the package.

He brought it up to his nose and sniffed. Sure enough, it was a ham.

Tucking the lumpy piece of pork under his arm, Austin flew into the dining room. Just as he'd hoped, Josephine already had the table set for dinner. Aunt Olivia was always hungry when she came in from an outing. Come to think of it, plump Aunt Olivia was always hungry—period.

But there was no time to smirk about that now. Austin selected a knife from the sideboard and set the ham on the platter. With shaking fingers, he unwrapped the paper and stared for a second at the sugary pink meat.

Kady said there were always instructions in the bone, he thought.

He had to find out. Without looking to see if a cut had been made to get the note in there, he drew back the carving knife and gave the ham a whack. It took several whacks before he found the bone, and then he had to massacre the ham to dig it out.

Those maroons must be better at this than I am, he thought.

Hands now gooey with meat fat, Austin poked his finger into the bone. A limp curl of paper fell out the other end.

Austin had to read only a few words to know these were instructions for some fugitive slave to get his freedom. Austin started to put his hand over his mouth, then pulled it away in distaste and took a moment to wipe his hands clean on a napkin.

What was to be done now? If he didn't get this to where it was supposed to be, someone was going to be disappointed—or worse. What if the maroon waited too long in his hiding place and was caught?

Frantically, Austin snatched up the paper the ham had been wrapped in and searched for writing on the inside. Kady had found *her* instructions there last time.

There were some words written faintly down in one corner. Austin's lips moved as he read silently, "Uncle Tom says if the roads are not too bad, you can look for those fleeces of wool by tomorrow. Send them on."

They always write in code, Austin thought. *Kady said that.* He considered the paper again. *"Fleeces of wool"—those must be the slaves. They'll be here tomorrow!*

Kady had to know. And she also had to know that somebody hadn't gotten the word that she no longer lived here. What if someone else in the house had gotten this package?

But they didn't—I did, Austin thought. *And I have to do something about it.*

He looked at the ham and felt himself sag. There was no way to use this butchered piece of meat to transport the message. He dumped the ham onto the serving platter and wiped the goo off the inside of the paper with another one of Aunt Olivia's linen napkins.

What to do with this now? he thought. *This is so hard to do alone.*

But getting help from Henry-James was out of the question, even if he had been there. He'd made a vow to be good and stay out of trouble. Austin couldn't argue with that.

Stuffing the fouled napkins into a drawer in the sideboard, Austin tore off the corner of the paper with the writing on it, hid the rest of it behind an urn, and rolled the important part around his finger.

The question now was where to put it.

"What would Kady do?" Austin whispered to himself. "She's so good at this!"

And then he remembered something. He'd lain in bed that night and watched her roll that piece of paper up into her hair.

Austin reached for his own head and then grunted at himself. *I don't have enough hair to hide a piece of straw in!* he thought.

Who had a lot of hair? Certainly not Polly, with her lifeless little curls, and she was out coaching anyway.

Well then, who?

As he heard the dancing footsteps coming down the stairs, he knew just exactly who.

He ran to the dining room door and poked his head out. Charlotte stood before him, dressed in the almost-to-her-ankles blue dress with the flounced skirts and stiffened petticoats that Aunt Olivia had given her for Christmas. She was wearing black shiny dancing slippers and had her deer-colored hair pulled into curls at the back of her neck. She looked much older than her 11 years.

"Perfect!" he said.

Her cheeks turned pink. "You think so?"

"Yes! Here, Lottie, can you put this in your hair?"

He handed her the roll of paper.

She stared at it for a moment, and Austin thought she looked a little disappointed, though he couldn't for the life of him figure out why. But her eyes lit up the way they always did when she and Austin were about to have an adventure, and she said, "Another message for a maroon?"

Austin nodded.

"It smells like ham," she said.

"Never mind that. Just roll it up in your hair, and I'll explain on the way."

"Where are we going?" she said as Austin pulled her toward the door.

"We're going to look for Kady," he said.

Charlotte nodded, but her eyes suddenly grew big.

"What's the matter?" Austin said. "Come on."

"Not this way. We have to go out the back. Don't you hear the carriage?"

Even as she said it, a clip-clopping of horses' hooves grew louder on the cobblestone street.

"All right," Austin whispered—as if they could hear him. "Out the side door to the piazza and over the railing. We'll hide in the bushes."

"Hurry!"

They slipped and slid their way through the drawing room and out the French doors that led to the side piazza. Charlotte was careful to close them behind her, but Austin dove for the railing. In his usual gangly fashion, he got over it and fell headlong into the camellia bushes below. He stuck up his hand to help Charlotte, but she hiked easily over and down in a flurry of petticoats and squatted down beside him—just before the carriage clattered past.

"Why did they come back this way?" Austin whispered frantically to Charlotte. "Why didn't Henry-James let the ladies out in front?"

"Who cares?" Charlotte said. "Sometimes you ask entirely too many questions, Boston."

But Charlotte was grinning as she peered through the bushes and gave Austin the all-clear sign. It had been a long time since he'd seen her look so excited, or felt that way himself. He still remembered to say a quick prayer as they crept out of the bushes and then charged up the sidewalk toward Tradd Street.

I hope this is right, Jesus, he thought. *Because we're doing it!*

"Do you remember where the warehouse is?" Charlotte whispered over her shoulder.

"I'm not sure," Austin whispered back.

Jesus must have been listening, Austin thought, because after only a few false turns, the warehouse suddenly loomed in front of them. Charlotte slowed to a walk, and Austin felt her shiver.

"It's a spooky-looking place," she said.

Austin had to agree. He had the hair-raising feeling on his arms again.

"Do you think anybody followed us?" he said.

"There was no one at home *to* follow us," Charlotte said. She shook her head firmly. "We're just getting the willies because of this awful place." She took a deep breath and straightened her blue-ruffled shoulders. "Let's just go."

"I hope Kady's in there," Austin said.

If she was, she was the only one. Although the wharves themselves were alive with the usual people dropping off and picking up shipments, the warehouse was deserted. It looked for all the world as if no one had been there since Henry-James and Austin had peeked through the window. The same clear space they'd made on the glass was still there.

"I should wait outside to keep watch," Austin said. "Will you be all right in there alone?"

Charlotte didn't look entirely sure, but she nodded and patted the bun at the base of her neck.

"It looks fine," Austin said. "No one will be able to tell—and you look at least 16."

Charlotte looked pleased as she disappeared inside the door. He knew he would never figure out girls.

Austin wanted to peek in the window in the worst way. But it was better not to, he decided. Better not to look too suspicious. Still, how noticeable would it be, he wondered, to walk to the corner of the building and have a look around the side, just to be sure no one was lurking about? He still had that sinister feeling. This place really did give one the gooseflesh.

Trying not to look obvious—Kady had told him not ever to try to be a spy—he walked casually along the building to the corner. Tugging at his jacket as if all he had to do that day was keep his clothes neat, he then leaned around the corner.

He felt a wave of relief. He didn't see a soul anywhere.

And after that, he didn't see anything—at all. There was a sharp pain in his head, and then everything went black.

✦ ⬥ ✦

Chapter Fifteen

"**I**t was pitiful, is what it was," Austin heard someone say. The voice sounded smoky.

No, it was the room that was smoky, he realized. The voice was coming out of someone's nose, as if he had very thin nostrils.

Where am I? Austin thought.

He opened his eyes, but the wisps of smoke stung them. Was the room burning?

He sniffed, and then he wrinkled his nose, which made his head ache. It was tobacco he smelled. And pain he felt. Why wasn't anybody doing anything about the pain in his head?

He tried again to open his eyes. As he did, he heard another voice say, "Have you checked on our hostage?"

"He's still out cold," said still another man in a brusque tone. "He won't be able to ask any questions for a while—thank the Lord."

"He's as bad as his father with the questions," said the man with the nasal voice. "I'll be glad to be rid of them both."

"But we need them both right now. And we've got them."

There was an ugly chorus of snickers. Austin squeezed his eyes shut and lay as still as he could.

153

Those are familiar voices, he thought. *I know these men— and they obviously know me.*

But his head was throbbing, and the smoke was clouding his thoughts. He couldn't seem to put two and two together.

"So you saw it, did you, the attack?" said the man with the abrupt way of putting his words.

"I did," said Nose. "Luckiest day of my life." He chuckled. "I knew, of course, that there were Confederate soldiers on Morris Island—"

"Wait, let me get the sound of that." The man speaking talked with a wheeze.

I know that voice, Austin thought. But he was still too confused to put a name to it. Even if he'd been able to think of it, he couldn't have said it. He realized for the first time that there was a piece of cloth tied around his mouth.

"Say it again—'Confederate'," the man went on.

"You're a simple thing, aren't you, Chesnut?" said Nose.

Chesnut!

A picture burst into Austin's head, setting it to pounding again. It was the three of them—the Fire Eaters. Virgil Rhett with his clipped tone. Roger Pryor who talked through his nose. Lawson Chesnut who couldn't say two words without running out of breath. What on earth was he doing with them?

"That's what we are now," Roger Pryor was saying. "We're not Americans—we're Confederates."

"Go on," Rhett said curtly. "What did the Confederates do?"

"They saw that steamship coming, and they knew it was headed right for Fort Sumter. Do those Union people think we're stupid?"

Chesnut wheezed out a laugh. "Well, we're not!"

"Trying to get supplies to Fort Sumter, were they?" Rhett barked.

"Of course they were, and in an unarmed vessel—a passenger

boat—*Star of the West* or some such name."

Austin nearly bolted from the bed. He had to grab onto a bolster to hold himself in place. *Star of the West! What happened to it?* he wanted to cry.

"So there were our Confederate soldiers on Morris Island," Pryor went on, "ready in the redoubts when she drew near. And then—boom!—they fired on her."

No!

"Didn't sink her, did they?" Rhett said.

"Didn't try. Just scared her off. She turned and run like a rabbit out to sea. She's on her way back to New York right now."

Austin's soul dropped like a ball of lead. His father had been so close—right there in Charleston Harbor. And now he was headed in the opposite direction. For all that he hated the thought of leaving his friends, Austin felt a longing for his father that cut deeply into him.

Chesnut was gasping out a gale of laughter. "I knew President Buchanan was a fool, but I never took him for *that* much of a clown! Sending an unarmed vessel down here!"

"Well," Roger Pryor said. Austin could almost picture him jerking back his long hair and looking down his pointy nose. "We're just lucky Lincoln hasn't been inaugurated yet. Don't think for a minute *he's* going to be that stupid."

"I don't think it's going to matter," Virgil Rhett snapped. "With as little as he has out there, Major Anderson is either going to have to give up Fort Sumter or starve there."

"Huh," Chesnut said. He stopped and breathed in, as if he were sucking in on a pipe. "I wonder if Wesley Hutchinson is going to be that stupid when he comes to rescue his son."

"I don't care how stupid he is," said Rhett, "as long as he comes and we nab him. I've been wanting to get my hands on that bloody abolitionist for a long time!"

"Shhh!" Chesnut said. "You'll wake the little mongrel up."

"You don't wake someone up from unconsciousness," said Pryor. "*Now* who's stupid?"

They sniggered and smoked and chattered some more. Austin didn't listen to them. He'd heard all he needed to hear.

I've been kidnapped, he thought. *I'm like a lure. I'm going to bring Father right into their hands!*

Pain tore across his chest and nudged him to panic.

I can't lose my head. They won't hurt me, he assured himself over and over. *They need me to get to Father. We have to warn him! He can't walk into this trap!*

That was what it was, of course—not an adventure and certainly not a game. This was a trap, and he didn't see how he was going to get out of it.

It was suddenly almost impossible not to hurl himself from the bed and throw himself at the feet of this nasty Vigilance Committee and beg them to let him go.

We'll go back north and never come here again! he'd cry, even through his gag.

I can't do that, Austin thought. *Glory, this must be the narrow gate for sure!*

He closed his eyes tighter and tried to think. Should he pretend to be dead? Make a run for the door? Throw some kind of fit so they'd have to call a doctor?

He'd been fumbling for a solution for only a few minutes when the voices from across the room drifted back to him through the smoke.

"You've sent the message to Hutchinson, then?" Virgil Rhett said.

"I have. Last I heard he was in New York. He's not just lecturing and writing now. I've heard he's trying his hand at helping fugitive slaves."

"He'll give all that up once he gets our wire," Chesnut wheezed. And then he snorted a laugh in and out. " 'Your presence for your son's life, Hutchinson!' Ha ha!"

Austin's mind spun. *"Your presence for your son's life."* If *Father doesn't come, I'll be killed. They'll kill me.*

It wasn't hard to believe—not from the sound of their voices as they cut his father to ribbons across their card table. He was sure it would have driven him right off the bed screaming "No! Leave us alone!" if there hadn't been a knock at the door.

"Who could that be?" Virgil Rhett muttered. "No one knows we're here."

"I certainly didn't tell my wife!" Chesnut said, still snorting.

"See who it is," Roger Pryor said.

Someone scraped back a chair and went to the door. There was a stiff silence as the door creaked open.

"Oh," Roger Pryor said. "What is it?"

"I've been sent to tidy up," said a small female voice.

"Who sent you?"

"Come in," Roger Pryor called out. Austin could almost picture him giving Rhett a steely eye. One way to look suspicious was for a "gentleman" to be openly rude to servants. Most of the time, they just ignored them.

They seemed to do just that, because they went back to muttering to each other, and he could hear the door closing and the tiny footsteps of a girl moving around the room. Austin felt a glimmer of hope. Perhaps he could give this girl some kind of signal that he was in trouble, and she could send help.

Stealthily, as if they were trapdoors, he opened his eyes a slit.

And then he opened them wide and stifled a gasp.

It was Lottie!

Dressed in a black maid's uniform that made her look even older than she had a few hours earlier, she was moving slowly and methodically around the room with a feather duster. But her eyes weren't on what she was doing. She was studying the place like it was a history text.

"That's enough tidying up now," Rhett said.

"That will be all," Roger Pryor agreed through his nose. "You can run on then."

Even though Lottie took the order and left the room, Austin's heart took a giant leap upward. *She saw me—I'm sure she saw me*, he kept telling himself. *Help is on the way!*

The trick now was to keep the men from becoming suspicious. He listened hard, but they didn't mention the maid again.

"What are we going to do with him when he comes to?" Chesnut said.

"Keep that gag on him, first off," Rhett said. "I never saw a boy could talk as much as he does."

"I tell you," Chesnut said, "he gets it from his father."

There was another knock at the door. Austin heard someone slap his hand on the tabletop. He strained hard to listen.

"What on earth? What is going on here?" Virgil Rhett said.

"Stay calm, man," Pryor said. "This is a hotel. There're going to be people coming and going. Settle down."

Rhett harrumphed, and it sounded from the heavy thudding on the floor like Lawson Chesnut was going to the door this time.

"What's this?" he said, groping for air.

"Your trunk, sir," said a voice Austin knew well. "The trunk you done sent for?"

"We didn't send for any trunk!" Rhett cried.

Austin could barely keep from laughing out loud. It was Henry-James, and he was evidently hauling a trunk into the room because the men sent up a whole round of protests.

"We didn't send for a trunk!"

"Get this fool thing out of here!"

"Who told you we wanted a trunk?"

Through it all, Henry-James played dumb as dust.

"I's jus' been tol' to bring this here trunk to this here room, and that's what I done. And if'n I don't, I's gonna be in a heap o' trouble. Please don't make no trouble for me, massa, please don't. If'n I don't deliver this here trunk, I's gonna be whipped to within a inch of my life!"

"Don't you leave this here!" Chesnut gasped.

"I gots to, massa," Henry-James said.

Austin could tell he was leaving. His footsteps disappeared, and the three Fire Eaters kept shouting after him.

"Oh, for heaven's sake!" Pryor said. "Chesnut, why did you pick this hotel?"

"Did you want me to put us up at the Mills House with everyone and his brother passing through?" Chesnut said. Austin could picture his nostrils flaring defensively.

"All right," Pryor said. "Rhett, why don't you go downstairs and see if you can straighten out this mess?"

Rhett went out, still muttering under his breath. Austin wanted desperately to open his eyes and see what the other two were doing. But he couldn't risk it. He had to think.

Why did Henry-James bring a trunk up here? he thought. *It's for me, that's sure. But what's in it? Am I supposed to get a weapon out of it or something?*

No, Henry-James would never do that. He'd seen Austin wield a hunting rifle. Somebody was likely to get killed!

And then, of course, it came to him, as obvious as the multiplication tables. A trunk—for Austin to climb into, just like the fugitive slaves did.

The question was, how? He dared open one eye until he could just see. Pryor and Chesnut were examining the trunk and mumbling to each other about its being empty. Harmless mistake obviously, they said.

"Let's get it out of here," one of them said to the other.

No! Austin thought in a panic. *Don't take it out yet!*

"Help! Help me, someone! Help!"

The voice was coming from outside, but it was so loud and

high-pitched that it even shrieked its way in through the closed window. Through his partially opened eye, Austin saw the two men hurry to open their window and lean out over the street below. It was safe to watch, and Austin did.

Because it didn't take two words for him to know that the voice below was coming from Kady.

⁘ ⬦ ⁘

Chapter Sixteen

"Y̶ou, up there! Can you give a girl a hand here? I'm in trouble, I am!"

Kady was using her Irish accent, and Austin was glad he had a gag to keep him from laughing.

"What's the matter, girl?" Chesnut called down to her. "What are you caterwaulin' about down there?"

"Help!" she screeched. "Somebody help!"

Good grief! Austin thought. *She sounds like Aunt Olivia!*

"Shut the window," Roger Pryor said. "That Irish wench is breaking my eardrums!"

"No, don't! I need help!"

"Then what's the matter with you? Tell us what's wrong!"

"Look for yourselves!" the Irish Kady screamed back.

Lean out the window and look, Austin thought. He opened his eyes to slits. That's exactly what they were doing—Chesnut going so far that Austin was sure he'd get his pudgy body stuck in the window frame.

With their backs to him and their attention turned to Kady's carryings-on below, it was as if the Fire Eaters had given Austin an open invitation. Moving carefully to keep the bed springs from squeaking, he maneuvered the feather bolster down alongside his body. Then he slid out of his jacket and knickers and dressed the big pillow. He hoped that at a glance it would look like him lying there.

Now came the tricky part. To get to the trunk, lift the lid, slip in, and close it again without their noticing was going to take a miracle.

For the moment, Chesnut and Pryor were still craning their upper bodies out the window, and Kady, bless her, continued to wail like a woman selling oysters in the marketplace. Austin hopped soundlessly off the bed and crept behind the wing chair that was just beside the trunk.

"Why don't you call a policeman?" Chesnut cried. He was wheezing more than ever, what with the windowsill cutting into his sizable belly.

"Can't you see I'm helpless?" Kady called back.

"No!" Pryor shouted. "I can't see that at all. You've got the lung power of an elephant!"

"I've been robbed!" Kady cried. "Go after them!"

"Go after who?"

But there was only a fresh refrain of screeching. Austin peeked out from behind the chair. Pryor and Chesnut were making moves as if to pull themselves back in.

No! Austin thought frantically. *Just give me another minute.*

But there wasn't going to be one, that was plain. Sucking in his breath, Austin reached out a hand and got his fingers between the lid and the trunk. Working them like inchworms, he got the trunk lid open about an inch. Then he stuck out his other arm, got the fingers of his other hand in the crack and held them at the ready.

On the count of three, he promised himself. *One, two—*

Thinking *three*, he made a move. But the chair slid, banging into the front of the trunk and sending the lid pressing down on both sets of fingers. He chomped back a cry and clamped his eyes shut.

"What was that?" he heard Pryor say.

"Oh, no, here they come again," Kady screamed. "They're coming! Please, help me!"

"She's a mad one," Pryor said. "Chesnut, go for the hotel manager—"

"Don't leave, please!"

There was just no more time to waste. Fingers still smarting, Austin steered clear of the chair, shuffled on his knees to the trunk, and slowly opened the lid.

When the opening was just big enough for him to get through, he did, one leg at a time. He wished his heart would stop beating so hard so he could hear better.

But as he lowered the lid over his head, it didn't sound as if either Lawson Chesnut or Roger Pryor had noticed that their hostage was no longer on the bed.

Now what? Austin thought. He felt around him. *Lord, please send somebody quick. It's dark in here.*

It most assuredly was. Not so much as a crack of light filtered through—and whatever had lived in this trunk before hadn't smelled any too good. The odor of camphor balls and sweat mixed in his nose and made him want to gag. He pulled the cloth off his mouth and held it over his nose.

I don't know how the maroons do it for hours and hours and miles and miles. They must really want their freedom.

It was a sobering thought, one that made him squeeze himself into a little ball and pray hard. The excitement that had tingled in him when he and Charlotte had set off on their adventure a few hours before was soggy and heavy in him now. All he wanted was to get out of this room and out of this trunk—and get to a place where somehow he could warn his father.

The pounding on the door was like a song in his ears.

"What on earth?" Roger Pryor cried out. "Is this City Hall?"

There was a rustling and a bumping out in the room. Austin did manage a grin at the thought of Lawson Chesnut trying to pry himself out of the window. Once more, the door was flung open, and a full, male voice—with an Irish brogue—belted out into the room.

"Excuse me, gentlemen," Fitz Kearney said. "I think there's been a mistake. Did my boy deliver a trunk to this room? Oh, glory be, there it is!"

"That's your trunk?" Roger Pryor said through his nose.

"Aye, sir, it is. And when I get my hands on that colored boy, he'll pay, by Jove! Do you mind, then?"

"No!" Chesnut gasped out. "Get the thing out of here. And if that Irish woman in the street is yours, take her, too!"

"She's none of mine!" Fitz said. "I wouldn't have the likes of her!"

Austin felt a jolt, and he knew strong-armed Fitz was hoisting the trunk up onto his shoulders. Austin felt for something to hold on to, but there was nothing. He pressed his feet against one side, his hands against the other, and stiffened his body. When the trunk went high into the air, he didn't move. It was a nauseating feeling, but he was too relieved to even think about throwing up.

"I thought she belonged to you," Fitz went on as he carried the trunk across the room. "The way she's been hollering up to you, I think you're the only ones who are going to be able to shut her up."

"You go check, Chesnut," Pryor said. "I'll stay here and—"

He stopped, and so did Austin's heart. Had he already discovered that Austin was no longer on the bed?

"What have you got to do that's so important?" Fitz said. "You'll have a whole hotel full of people obliged to ya if you'll take care of the lass right away!"

Pryor muttered, and Austin heard two sets of footsteps following them out of the room.

"What's the matter with her, does anyone know?" Fitz said.

"Somethin' about somebody bein' after her," said Chesnut.

"The people from the insane asylum, would be my guess," Fitz said, laughing. "You'd be doin' us all a service if you took her there, eh?"

Chesnut and Pryor didn't laugh. But once Austin felt them getting to the bottom of the stairs, their footsteps did veer off in another direction.

Fitz hesitated only a moment before he whispered, "Are you all right in there?"

"Yes!" Austin whispered back. "Are they gone?"

"Aye! And so are we!" He started to run. "You nearly cooked our goose, lad. You surely did!"

"I'm sorry!" he wanted to cry. But he had to concentrate, to press harder to keep from being bounced back and forth. There was a loud thud as the bottom of the trunk hit something. A few minutes later, Austin heard the creaking of a wagon and felt the rocking.

"Halt! You there—in the wagon!" someone cried.

It was the unmistakable nasal voice of Roger Pryor, screaming as if he were running after them. Both the wagon and Austin's heart began to move faster. They obviously careened around a corner because the trunk slid crazily and slammed against something hard. Austin guessed it was the side of the wagon. Another turn and it slid back the other way. This time Austin's head banged against the inside of the trunk, and he couldn't help crying out. His poor head was beginning to feel like a rug must feel when Mousie was pounding the dust out of it.

But at last the cries of the Fire Eaters faded out, and the wagon slowed down, its noises mixing with the sounds of Charleston—the *Mercury* carrier yelling about his news, the bells on the Baptist Church chiming out the hour, trains tooting and chuffing on all sides of him.

And then even that trailed off behind them. There was nothing except for the solitary cawing of a crow and the rapid clopping of the horse's hooves. All Austin could hear were the thoughts in his own head: *Hurry! We have to warn Father! Hurry!*

And, *It's my fault! It's all my fault—again!*

Fresh air had never smelled so good to Austin as finally, when the wagon had stopped and the trunk had been lifted out and carried some more and set down, the lid was opened. Austin blinked up at the welcome face of Henry-James.

"You're safe!" Austin said. At least there was that.

"I is," Henry-James said. He took Austin's arm and pulled him out of the trunk. But he also scowled and stepped back into a corner, folding his hands and looking respectfully at the floor.

"You don't need to be doin' any of that, lad," Fitz said to him as he took off his cap and hung it on the hook by the door. "This is my house—mine and Kady's now. We treat everybody equal here. Come on, then, have a seat."

"Where are we?" Austin said.

"We're outside Charleston—way up past Moultrie Street." Fitz shook his head a little. "We do our best to keep out of the sight of the townspeople, what with all the comin' and goin' of strange packages."

Austin stretched his cramped legs. "Where's Kady? And Charlotte?"

"They ought to be comin' along any minute now." Fitz peeked out the muslin curtain. "Kady's a sly one. She'll give those mongrels the slip. That's my girl!" He looked at them, grinning, eyebrows going up and down.

Any other time, Austin would have been studying the room. As it was, he only noticed that it was small and old and, though tidy and cheerful, there wasn't a piece of rosewood Gothic

Victorian furniture in sight. Aunt Olivia, he knew, would be turning up her nose.

But he didn't give it much thought. His chest was aching—over Charlotte and Kady, and most of all, his father.

"I have to tell you what those men said when they thought I was unconscious," Austin said.

"Aye, I want to hear it all," said Fitz. He tilted his red head and held up a finger. "In a minute. I think the lassies have arrived."

"It's them, all right, massa," Henry-James said. "I can hear a horse."

"Henry-James," Fitz said, "how long is it going to take you to stop calling me 'master'? You helped save *our* hides today, remember? I should be kissin' your feet, eh? Let me see one of those!"

He made a dive as if he were actually going to smother one of Henry-James's feet with slobbery lips, but a horse clattered abruptly to a stop outside, and Fitz's attention turned to the door. Austin could tell Henry-James was grateful for that. His face was shiny with embarrassment . . . and some pride, too.

Austin himself felt pretty ashamed.

I've got nothing to be proud of, he thought miserably. *If I'd been more careful, none of this would have happened. We have to warn Father now!*

The front door was flung open, and the Ravenal girls blew in, skirts swirling and cheeks flushed. Charlotte saw Austin and ran to him like a frightened chick.

"Are you all right?" she said. "Did those miserable pieces of pigflesh hurt you? No, *pig* is too good for them! I like our *sows* better than I do them—"

"Never mind that!" Austin burst out. He couldn't hold it in any longer. "We have to get a message to Father! I have to warn him!"

"About what?" Kady said. "Talk to us, Austin."

With all the eyes on him, so full of concern and fear, Austin's voice started to shake. "They said they sent a message to Father to lure him into South Carolina to rescue me," he said. "It's going to be waiting for him when the *Star of the West* gets back to New York!"

"I heard about the attack," Kady said. She looked at Fitz, who was thoughtfully rubbing his nose with his index finger.

"It could take some time for them to get back," he said. "It gives me a chance to beat them to the punch."

"What does that mean?" Charlotte said.

"That means your Uncle Wesley will never get that message, lassie," Fitz said, "not if I have anything to do with it."

He went to Kady and, sweeping her up off her feet, began to whisper to her. Austin immediately turned away. Chances were, they'd be kissing any minute. And besides, his eyes were starting to film over.

"Don't worry," Charlotte said. "I think Fitz and Kady can do just about anything."

Austin nodded. He didn't trust himself to speak. Henry-James, on the other hand, had plenty to say.

"Massa Austin, we gots to get home. Once Marse Drayton and yo' mama notice you ain't there, there gonna be big troubles."

Charlotte nodded solemnly. "There are enough of those already. Maybe Kady will let us borrow the wagon."

"Nothing doing," Kady said.

The front door closed softly as Fitz left. Kady wrapped her cape tightly around herself. "Come on, you three. I'm taking you back to the townhouse myself."

"But what if Daddy—or Mama—sees you?" Charlotte said.

"I'll take that chance. But I'm not going to let you go all the way back there alone. You've been through enough today."

Charlotte and Henry-James nodded and went for the door.

Austin stayed, head hanging. The floor swam in front of him.

"We need to hurry, you know," Kady said to him. "I'd like to get you back there before anyone realizes you're gone. Although you're certainly hard not to miss." She stopped and put her hand on Austin's shoulder. "What is it, my friend? This isn't like you."

"It's my fault," Austin said. "I was trying to go through the narrow gate, and I guess I'm just not good enough for that. I'm not good like Daddy Elias."

"What on earth are you talking about?" Kady asked. "Is this some kind of riddle I'm supposed to figure out?"

Austin shook his head and blinked hard. "I thought I was helping."

"You did help! Our little fleeces are already on their way to market, if you know what I mean."

"But my father might be on his way to 'market,' too—and now Fitz has to put himself in danger."

"Fitz *loves* to be in danger, Austin," Kady said. "And besides, don't you think those Fire Eaters have been looking for a chance to nab you—or Jefferson? It was only a matter of time. Now you'll know to be more careful."

Austin looked at her through the blur in his eyes.

"Listen," Kady said, "I don't know what narrow gate you're talking about, but it seems to me you're going through it just fine."

Austin shrugged. "I don't think so."

"Well, come on, you're going to find the narrowest gate yet if my mother catches Charlotte out at this hour!"

Austin didn't feel any lighter of heart as they made their way in the now familiar wagon. Kady let Henry-James sit up front with her, but she hid Austin and Charlotte under the blanket in the back once more. While they rode, Charlotte explained how they'd found Austin at the hotel.

"When I went in the warehouse and gave the message to Fitz," she said, "he was worried, and he wanted to talk to you himself to ask you some questions about the messenger who came to the door. But when we got outside, you were gone."

"I got hit over the head," Austin said. He rubbed it and felt something dried and scabby.

"I told Fitz something awful like that must have happened, but he wanted to believe you'd just run home scared." Austin could almost feel Charlotte rolling her honey-brown eyes in the darkness. "I told him you would never do anything like that."

"You did?" Austin said.

"Well, of course." She gave him a poke. "You may be clumsy and sometimes you talk too much, but, Boston, you are about the bravest and smartest boy I ever knew."

Austin gave a soft grunt. Then why didn't he *feel* very brave or smart—or good?

"Anyway," Charlotte went on, "he made me go home and check just in case. Mama and her company were in the drawing room having tea, and Henry-James was pacing like a dog in a pen. He wouldn't let me go back to the warehouse without him. He said he was in charge of seeing after you, and if anything happened to you, he didn't want to be around anyway."

Austin felt the pang in his chest again. "I hope I didn't get him in trouble tonight."

"I don't think he cares a thing about that," Charlotte said. "He sure forgot about it when we got to the warehouse, and Kady had arrived talking about the *Star of the West,* and Fitz had found a trail of blood."

"Blood?"

"Your blood, silly. You haven't seen the back of your head. They smacked you a good one."

"There are going to be questions about that at home," Austin said.

"Ria will fix it."

"Not when she finds out I put Henry-James in danger."

"Do you want to hear the story or not?"

Austin wasn't sure he did. This just seemed to be getting worse and worse. But Charlotte went on anyway.

"We followed the blood to where some buggy tracks started. We followed them as long as there was dirt road, and Fitz said he knew right where they'd taken you. To the St. Charles Hotel."

Austin's curiosity won out. "How did he know that?"

"He and Kady said that's where the Vigilance Committees were hiding out and making their plans. They followed them there the night you and Aunt Sally and Jefferson were supposed to sail for the North. That's how he and Kady knew to stop you—they overheard the men talking."

"So they dressed you up like a maid!" Austin said.

"Kady got the idea because I already looked older with my hair pulled up. I was scared, though, Boston. I thought surely they would recognize me."

"Not a chance," Austin said. "Like I told you, you looked 16."

"Really?" she said.

"Go on," Austin said.

"When I saw you there on the bed, I thought you were dead for sure. I almost went right up to that awful Roger Pryor and stomped on his foot!"

Austin suppressed a snicker.

"I wasn't going to leave until I was sure you were still alive. And then you opened that one eye. I wanted to grab your hand and pull you out of there, but Fitz told me just to be sure you saw me. Then you'd know to be ready."

"I was!"

"You know all about the rest. Fitz said he sure was glad you were smart enough to know to get into the trunk."

But Austin sagged again. "I should have been smart enough not to get into that mess in the first place. Kady says they would have found me someplace anyway, but—"

"She's right, Austin!"

But Austin still wasn't convinced. This narrow gate—he wasn't sure he was fit to go through it after all.

It may have been his most disturbing thought yet, worse than war or kidnapping or his father being lured into South Carolina.

"Austin, what's wrong?" Charlotte whispered. "I don't like it when you're quiet like that. It scares me."

But Austin couldn't reassure her. For once in his life, he just didn't know what to say.

It was growing colder as they finally arrived at White Point Garden and Kady reached into the wagon and pulled their blanket back. For the first time, she chuckled.

"What's funny?" Austin said.

"We were all so preoccupied, none of us noticed that you're in your undershirt and drawers! What have you done with your clothes?"

Austin groaned. "I dressed the bolster in them so they wouldn't notice at first that I was gone!"

"How clever of you!" she said. She laughed deep down in her throat. "I wish I could be there to hear how you explain *this!* I miss your endless, complicated stories, Austin."

For a moment, she looked as if she missed a lot more than that. Whitened by the moonlight and the strain of the day, her face was pale and drawn, and her big chocolatey eyes dark and drooping. Life might be an adventure for Kady right now, Austin thought, but she was sad, too. It made him angrier than ever at Aunt Olivia and Uncle Drayton.

And it was that anger that hauled him out of the wagon and straightened his shoulders as he and Charlotte and Henry-James started off toward the townhouse.

"Try not to tell Daddy that I was involved today," she whispered after them. "But if you have to, I'll understand. Just get a message to the warehouse if you have to tell."

I may have made a mess of things today, Austin thought as they hurried toward the house on East Bay, *but I won't make trouble for Kady. She's protected me, and I'm going to protect her—no matter what.*

Please help me, Jesus.

And then they pushed open the side door and walked right into the waiting arms of Uncle Drayton . . . a very red-faced, angry Uncle Drayton.

✝ ✝ ✝

Chapter Seventeen

t first, Uncle Drayton didn't say a word. He only stood towering over Charlotte with eyes glinting like pieces of metal in the sun. Austin sneaked a glance at the rest of the drawing room. They were all there, including Ria. Austin's heart started to dip again, but he forced himself to stand tall with his shoulders squared.

"It wasn't Charlotte's fault," he said. "It was mine."

"Oh!" Aunt Olivia shrieked from the chaise longue. "He's in his ... unmentionables!"

She waved her hands in front of her face like a flustered chicken flapping its wings until Mousie produced the inevitable handkerchief and Aunt Olivia covered her eyes with it.

Uncle Drayton ignored Austin and turned on Henry-James. "And you! I ordered you to keep watch over these children—"

"He did!" Austin said. "He's the reason we're back safe. I was kidnapped!"

"Oh, for heaven's sake!" Uncle Drayton's voice blared out like a trumpet blown too hard. "That is the worst lie you have told yet!"

"I'm not lying," Austin said. "It was the Fire Eaters—Pryor and Chesnut and Rhett. They hit me over the head." He twisted his head and pointed to the spot with the dried blood. "And then they took me to the St. Charles Hotel." He searched the room for his mother, who was clutching Jefferson on her lap so hard that Austin was surprised the boy's eyes didn't pop out. "They sent a message to Father to come and rescue me or they'd kill me."

"We have to warn him!" Mother cried.

"Somebody is already on the way to do that," Austin said.

"Who would you know to send?" Uncle Drayton said.

"I can't tell you—"

"Austin, out of my sight! I haven't time for your cockamamy stories tonight."

"Drayton, hush up." Everyone in the room stared as one at Sally Hutchinson. She was glaring at her brother, her Ravenal eyes unblinking. "How many times does Austin have to prove to you that he is trustworthy? I want to hear what he has to say."

Uncle Drayton's eyes blazed back at his sister. For a long minute, their gazes burned back and forth as if they were going up and down a smoldering rope that the two of them held taut. An entire, unspoken conversation seemed to take place before Uncle Drayton's shoulders drooped and he walked slowly across the drawing room to the table, where he pressed his palms flat and stared down at the shiny tabletop.

"Ria, he's ill!" Aunt Olivia said. "Go to him at once!"

But Uncle Drayton held up a hand. "I'm ill, Ria," he said, "but there's nothing you can do about it. My sickness comes from the miserable state of affairs that seems to have driven all reason out of my mind." He sighed heavily. "Austin, you say you've sent word to your father?"

"Someone has, yes, sir," Austin said.

Uncle Drayton nodded, his head still hanging, his back still to them. "And does this person have anything to do with Kady?"

Austin felt Charlotte go rigid beside him. His own chest throbbed, the fear was so intense. But he lifted his chin and said, "I can't tell you that, Uncle Drayton."

"Then that answers my question, doesn't it?" Uncle Drayton said. He stood up abruptly and turned to them. "If you will all excuse me." He started for the door, then stopped and leveled his eyes at Henry-James. "You," he said. "Come with me. I want my fire laid and my boots polished. Bring me a pot of chocolate as well."

"Yes, massa," Henry-James said. And with his eyes lowered to the floor, he left the room behind Uncle Drayton.

Without a word to anyone, Mother deposited Jefferson onto the floor and swept from the room, her head held high.

She's going through a narrow gate, too, Austin thought.

He followed her.

When he got to her room, she was pacing the floor and talking, although there wasn't another soul there.

"Who are you talking to?" Austin said.

"Your father . . . or God." She tossed her hands in the air. "Anyone who will listen! I have to make sure what I'm doing is right."

Austin went slowly to her bed and sat on it while he watched her meander in and out between the cots.

"Don't you know what's right?" he said. "I thought you always knew."

She stopped and looked at him as if he'd just grown an ear in the middle of his forehead. "Where on earth would you get an idea like that?" she said.

"Because," he said. He twisted his mouth for a second. "Because you're so good. Not like me."

All the anger seemed to drain out of Mother. By the time she got to the bed, her eyes were big and concerned.

"What are you saying?" she said. "You're not good? That is absurd, Austin."

Austin shook his head. "I try. I really do. I pray, but it always turns out all wrong. Now I've gotten Father in danger."

"Hold on there," she said. "You didn't do anything of the kind. It's those wretched Fire Eaters who are at fault, not you."

Still Austin shook his head, hard. "But if I didn't do stupid things—"

"What stupid things? Austin, you do wonderful things all the time, and you don't even know it. That's what makes them so good. They're like little gifts, right from God."

Austin blinked at her. "Like what?"

"Like convincing your uncle to let Ria stay with Daddy Elias. Can you imagine what it would have been like if he'd had to die all alone?"

Austin shook his head.

"Have you noticed that your little brother doesn't try to get attention anymore? He hasn't said one word about Fitz, and he was right there that night Fitz and Kady kept us from going to Fort Sumter. That's because he tries to be like you."

"He does?"

Mother smiled. "You try so hard, you say, but when you don't try so hard—when you just are who God made you to be—that's when He works His magic in you."

"It doesn't feel like that. Daddy Elias said he could just feel Jesus in him, telling him the right thing to do."

"Daddy Elias was also over 70 years old. You're 11. Give yourself some time."

"But I make so many mistakes!"

"Who doesn't? I have said some awful things to Uncle Drayton in the heat of anger. I'm always apologizing. But remember what Daddy Elias always told you—Jesus will be there with the right answers at the right time. Sometimes just in the nick of time."

Austin thought about that while his mother waited, hands patiently folded in her lap.

"I have two questions," he said at last.

"Okay. Number one."

"I don't feel like it's time to go yet. I think there's something else I'm supposed to do here—only I don't know what. Do you think God will keep us here until I can do . . . whatever it is?"

"If He truly wants you to do it, yes," she said. "I'm sure of it. Question two?"

Austin looked down at his hands. "Do you think I'll go to heaven and be with Jesus like Daddy Elias?"

He felt his mother's fingers on his chin as she lifted it up so she could look at him. "I have never been more certain of anything in my life," she said. "The way you believe in the Lord, there is simply no question."

"Believe?" Austin said. "That's all I have to do?"

She nodded. "Believing makes you do good things. That's all there is to it."

They sat for a long time, just thinking together. It seemed to wear Sally Hutchinson out. She fell into an exhausted sleep early that night, and Charlotte did the same beside her, and Jefferson, too, in his little cot.

But Polly was in the mood for talking. While Tot snorted in slumber on the floor, she squeezed between Austin's and Jefferson's cots with her knees pulled up under her nightgown and asked a torrent of questions.

"Kady's husband—is he very handsome? Are they very much in love? Does she look at him with stars in her eyes?"

"I don't know," Austin said, wriggling uncomfortably. "I don't know anything about those things."

"You'd better learn pretty soon, Austin Hutchinson," she said. "You're going to have girls making eyes at you, you know."

Austin snorted. "At me? Polly, that's the silliest thing I ever heard you say."

"Laugh if you want," she said. "But I was just saying that to Tot the other day. Wasn't I, Tot?"

Tot moaned in her sleep.

"I was pointing out to her how tall and handsome you're becoming. If you can learn to be quiet once in a while, you'll have the young ladies swarming around you."

"Ugh!" Austin said. He sat up in his cot. "I don't *want* the girls swarming around me!"

"Not now, but you will," Polly said, eyes narrowed wisely. "You don't have much money, of course, but that will change. I think you'll make something quite clever of yourself."

Austin was shaking his head, and Polly was ignoring him.

"Besides, you're kind. There aren't many kind men about these days."

She swallowed and suddenly looked uncomfortable. Austin didn't blame her. He was squirming himself.

"I did want to tell you this before you go," she continued. "You are the first person to ever really be nice to me, besides my mother and father, of course. If it weren't for you, Kady and Charlotte would still be treating me as if I were a leper. So . . . thank you." She gave her thin curls a final bounce and got up quickly. "Good night. Sweet dreams."

Austin lay back down on his cot and stared at the ceiling until he heard Polly's breathing go deep and even up in his mother's bed. It wasn't until he felt something wet in his right ear that he realized there were tears coming out of his eyes. He swiped at them impatiently, but they kept coming.

He almost thought he'd started to sob out loud when he realized the sound he was hearing wasn't coming from him. It was coming from the hall. Somebody out there was crying into a pillow.

Austin slipped out of bed and opened the door a crack. The house was silent except for the raspy, muffled sound of weeping. Right there on the floor, coming from Henry-James's pallet.

Austin shut the door behind him as he went to him. He squatted down beside the boy, but he saw only the back of his woolly black head.

"Henry-James," Austin whispered. "What's the matter?"

Henry-James's head jerked up, and he glared at Austin from

within the slits his eyes had swollen to. His tears were big and shiny against his skin.

"Go away, please, Massa Austin," he said. "Please."

"No," Austin said. "You'd sit beside me while I cried. I know you would. What's wrong? What happened?"

Henry-James flopped like a flounder to his back and dug angrily at his eyes with his fists until his shoulders stopped shaking. Austin was glad they did. His friend's sobs were so wretched that they were pulling tears out of him again.

"I don' know what to do, Massa Austin," he said. "I jus' don' know what to do."

"You always know what to do," Austin whispered. "You just think you don't right now, but I bet you do."

Henry-James shook his head. "I want Daddy 'Lias here to tell me. No, I don't, 'cause I know what he'd say—and I can't do that, Massa Austin. I can't do that!"

Austin rubbed his own chest. "What can't you do?"

"I can't do like Daddy 'Lias said and be a good slave and obey everything Massa Drayton done tol' me."

"You've been obeying him ever since the funeral," Austin said. "You followed me today, just like Uncle Drayton told you to do."

Henry-James shook his head again. "He weren't mad 'bout that. He said I done right. But I can't do what he askin' me to do now, Massa Austin. I can't tell him where to find Miz Kady. I done lied to him tonight!"

"Oh," Austin said.

Henry-James gnawed at his lip. Austin could see the agony in his eyes.

"I reckon I won't never see Daddy 'Lias again, not even in heaven," Henry-James said.

"No!" Austin said. "My mother just told me, all you have to do is believe—you know, love Jesus. That's all it takes to get to heaven, no matter how many mistakes you make."

"Daddy Elias wouldn't want to see me anyway," Henry-James said. "Not bein' a liar like I gots to be. But don't you see, Massa Austin, I can't do it. I gots to protect Miz Kady."

Austin nodded. "I know just what you mean. I have the same problem. I want to walk through the narrow gate and stay here, but—"

"But you's free, Massa Austin," Henry-James said. "I ain't free to decide. That's what I can't stand."

Austin closed his eyes. But that didn't shut out the image that sprang to his mind—the picture of himself in a trunk with his feet and hands pressed against the sides. Smelling camphor and sweat. Wondering if he would ever see daylight again.

He opened his eyes and looked at Henry-James. His black eyes had dimmed, and he let his elbow slide down until his head hit his ragged pillow once more. The black eyes closed, and his face went expressionless. It looked as if the spirit had gone right out of him.

It was the saddest moment Austin had ever known.

Things didn't get much happier in the two weeks that followed.

Mother, of course, looked as if she were sitting on a pin cushion all the time, waiting for word from Father.

"I just hope this war holds off," she would say in a voice that grew weaker each day, "until we know if he received the message."

But that didn't look hopeful. The day Uncle Drayton got his letter from Jefferson Davis was the blackest day of all.

"Jefferson Davis has resigned from the U.S. Congress," Uncle Drayton told them all at dinner. "He is still hoping for a peaceful resolution, but I don't know. . . ."

His voice trailed off as it did so often these days. There was very little left of the witty, charming planter Austin had met a year ago when he'd first come to Charleston—the man he'd tried so hard to imitate. Uncle Drayton was now stoop-shouldered, with dark rings under his eyes and a defeated look on his face. He had even stopped trying to convince the Fire Eaters to turn back toward peace.

"What is the use?" he said one day when he'd finished reading the *Charleston Mercury.* "The Confederacy has been officially formed in Montgomery, Alabama—and without the sanction of the people. I didn't vote for it. I don't know anyone who was even given the chance to except the politicians who have taken over and convinced us all that this is in our best interest!"

All over the South, local forces were seizing Union forts until only two remained in Federal hands. One of them was Fort Sumter. The only thing that gave him any hope was that his beloved Jefferson Davis was inaugurated as president of the new Confederacy, which now included Mississippi, Florida, Alabama, Georgia, Louisiana, and Texas, as well as South Carolina.

"Why is that good news, Drayton?" Aunt Olivia said, nervously fanning her chins at the supper table. "Does that mean he won't let us go to war?"

Uncle Drayton shook his head. "He has told the Union the South wants to be left alone. But if attacked, it will, of course, defend itself." He sighed heavily and pushed his chair back. "I will follow Jefferson Davis's lead, just as I always have."

"Where are you going now?" Aunt Olivia said.

Uncle Drayton barely turned to her as he left the dining room. "I am going to announce that to my fellow Charlestonians," he said. "Our life here has become hard enough. We do not need our neighbors hating us now."

Austin found himself asking "Marse Jesus" to help Uncle Drayton through *his* narrow gate.

But it was his own gate that loomed largest the morning he woke up to a great banging on the front door. It was so early that the stars were still out, and so early that he opened the door before anyone else.

There, wrapped in a cape with a hood pulled low over her face, was Kady.

"What are you doing here?" Austin whispered. "Aren't you afraid of your father?"

"I couldn't send anyone else with this message," she said. Her eyes were big and young-looking, as if this were something even she couldn't handle alone. "May I come in?"

"Kady Sarah!" Aunt Olivia cried from the staircase.

Austin looked back to see her groping for the banister as if she were going to faint. He rolled his eyes.

Mousie appeared from out of nowhere and helped her mistress down the stairs. Aunt Olivia seemed much less interested in seeing Kady than in making a grand entrance into the drawing room.

The rest of the family emerged, shocked and sleepy, from their rooms. Uncle Drayton came out of the library. Either he was up very early, or he had never gone to bed. From the circles under his eyes, Austin guessed he'd been up all night.

"Well, well, well," he said when he saw his oldest daughter. His voice was cold. "Our prodigal returns."

"I haven't returned, Daddy," Kady said, her voice subdued. "I came to bring Aunt Sally a message."

"Then go right back to your pauper!" Aunt Olivia screeched from the drawing room. "If you haven't come back to apologize to us, you just go on back to your little hovel!"

"Hovel?" Charlotte whispered in Austin's ear. "I liked it at her house."

"Me, too," Austin whispered back.

Kady looked stung, but she moved past everyone to get to her aunt, who was near the bottom of the staircase, face white as milk. She put out both of her hands to Kady.

"I have word for you," Kady said. "Uncle Wesley has received our message. He knows that Austin is safe. He won't try to come into South Carolina right now."

Mother closed her eyes and nodded. Austin felt as if his chest were crushing in. Two big feelings were colliding there. He was so relieved—and he was so scared.

"Well, Kady," Uncle Drayton said, "since you seem to know everything there is to know, are you going to tell us how Wesley is to get his family out of the South before we come to blows with the North?"

"I know how we can help them," Kady said. "That's another reason why I came."

Aunt Olivia's head poked out of the drawing room. "How?" she said. "Tell us!"

Kady turned to Mother once more. "Major Anderson is going to send the women and children who have been trapped at Fort Sumter all this time to New York, and the Confederacy is going to allow it. If you and the boys want to go, we can try to get you out to the island. It might be dangerous—"

"Whatever we do is going to be dangerous," Mother said. "I don't see how we can pass up this opportunity."

This is a narrow gate if I ever saw one! Austin thought.

But his mother wasn't finished. "The strain of all this has taken its toll on my health again, however," she said. "Ria and I have been talking, and neither of us thinks I am strong enough to make a journey right now." She turned to Uncle Drayton. "If you don't mind, Drayton, I would like to stay. I think my boys have a better chance of getting out without me bogging them down."

Austin's mouth fell open. "What do you mean?"

"I mean I want you to go without me, Austin," she said. "You and Jefferson must go north alone."

✞ ◆✞◆ ✞

Chapter Eighteen

"Go without you?" Austin said.

He knew he sounded stupid. She'd said it plainly enough. But it didn't seem real—it *couldn't* be real.

"I don't see that we have any other choice," his mother said. "If you stay here, one or both of you will be kidnapped unless we keep you under lock and key, and that won't do at all. And if I should fall ill again on the way to New York, who would take care of me and look after you boys?"

"I could do it!" Austin said.

"I'm sure you could. But I won't put that kind of responsibility on you. You've had to grow up far too fast as it is."

"Suppose you took Ria with you?" Uncle Drayton said.

Everyone stopped to consider that for a moment.

Then Aunt Olivia gasped. "And just how would she get back here?" she said, eyes indignant. "What if one of us were to succumb to the pox or something while she's gone? Sally Hutchinson isn't the only one who needs medical attention, you know!"

As if to prove it, she swooned slightly. No one paid any attention except Mousie.

"I will put one responsibility on you, Austin," Mother said, "and that is to take care of your brother and do everything you're told aboard the ship. There will be adults to watch over you—it won't be like traveling alone on a train, which I would never let you do. You'll be fine. I know you will." She looked at her brother. "He's proven that now."

"He has," Uncle Drayton said. For the first time in weeks, he smiled. "Austin, I think you will have that ship turned upside down and inside out by the time it reaches New York." And then his face softened. "You can do this. I don't know of another young man I could say that of."

"But . . . I don't know . . ." Austin stammered.

"Austin," Kady said, "I think this is that narrow gate you told me about. Daddy Elias would want you to do whatever it took to get you and Jefferson to safety."

But that would be his *gate!* Austin wanted to shout. *This isn't my gate—and I don't want to go through it!*

"Come along upstairs, boys," Sally Hutchinson said. "You have packing to do—again."

She gave Kady a wistful smile, and Kady smiled back, sadly.

"Have them ready by sunset," she said. "I'll be back for them."

Then she glanced at her parents, her eyes hopeful. Neither of them would look at her. She wrapped her cape around her and left.

Sally Hutchinson started up the stairs, but she stopped. "Drayton, Olivia," she said, "you are foolish, foolish people. Your daughter is right here in Charleston, and you won't give her the time of day. I'm about to send my children hundreds of miles away—alone—and I don't know when I shall see them again. What I wouldn't give to be in your shoes." She took Austin and Jefferson by the shoulders and ushered them upstairs. "Get your things together, and you can say your good-byes."

That was the last thing Austin wanted to do. Good-bye made

it seem too real. Going on with the day like it was any other—
that was what he wanted to do.

But it seemed that his leaving was everyone else's narrow
gate, and they were going to go through it the way they needed
to.

Polly was the first to appear, while Austin was sitting impatiently on the piazza waiting for Charlotte to come. Maybe they
could have one more adventure—

"I've already said my farewell to you, Austin," Polly said. "But
Tot wants to say hers."

Austin looked doubtfully at Tot, who was standing behind
Polly, twisting her starched apron in her fist. She looked as if
she'd rather be tied to the fence post than say anything, as far as
he could see.

"Go on, Tot," Polly said. "Tell him what you told me."

"You done treated me right, Massa Austin," Tot said in a voice
he could barely hear. "I's gonna miss you."

Her head proceeded to bob about a hundred times.

Polly looked hard at Austin. "Say something," she whispered.
"Before her head falls off!"

"Thank you, Tot," Austin said. "I hope . . . I hope you get free
someday."

Tot kept bobbing as she backed off and wandered into the
house. Polly stood there staring.

"You hope she gets free?" she said. "But what about me? What
would I do without her? With you gone, I don't have any friends
except her!"

To Austin's utter amazement, she turned with a tangle of petticoats and flew into the house.

What am I supposed to make of that? Austin thought.

There wasn't much time to make *anything* of it. He wanted
to find Charlotte. He went to his mother's room, but there was

only a napping Mother, as well as Ria, probably the last person he wanted to see.

But she was obviously anxious to see him. "I'm glad you come in, Massa Austin," she said. "I got somethin' to say to you."

Austin really wanted to turn on his heel and run—or at least say, "I'm leaving tonight, Ria. Why can't you just leave me alone? I'll never bother Henry-James again."

But he went over to the window where she was standing and waited. She folded her hands at her waist.

"You and me, we ain't always seen eye to eye, has we, Massa Austin?"

Austin shook his head.

"I reckon that's 'cause I didn't like them ideas you was always puttin' in Henry-James's head. Daddy Elias, he always say it don't do no harm. He say Massa Austin got his own walk to walk. But 'til this mornin', I jus' never could agree, no matter how many times I seen you do the right thing."

"What happened this morning?" Austin said.

"Your mama stand right there and she say she gon' let you go for your own good, even though she gots to stay behind. That there were the bravest thing I ever seen a person do. I reckon that's what I been missin' all this time. I gots to let go, too."

"I don't understand," Austin said.

"Then that be about the first time, ain't it?" she said.

There was a glimmer of a smile in her eyes, and for a tiny moment she brushed her hand against his arm.

"That's all I got to say, Massa Austin," she said. "Now, if'n you'll 'scuse me?"

Austin nodded, and she hurried over to the medicine table and began to clank spoons and bottles.

"Boston!" someone whispered from the doorway.

It was Charlotte. Her eyes were puffy and red, but there was a watery smile on her face.

Austin rushed to her and pushed her out into the hall with him.

"Where have you been?" he said. "We don't have much time left."

"Yes, we do—in a way," she said.

Austin had a ridiculously wonderful thought. "Are you coming with us?" he said.

"No, but it's the next best thing. I was crying so hard that I couldn't even come out of my room. Daddy found me in there, and he said that once a month—war or no war—I can get a message to you. I'll write a letter or send a wire or something, just as long as you always let me know where you are. And then you can make good on your Christmas promise and write me back. You can keep things to tell me in your little book I gave you. It won't be like never seeing each other again!"

She looked like she was hanging on to the last string that could hold a happy thought in her head. Austin couldn't snip it off, not for the world.

But getting a message from Charlotte once a month? When they'd had so many adventures together, when they'd shared secrets nobody else knew, when they'd seen each other cry and be hateful and still liked each other—next to all of that, a message once a month was like a single cake crumb.

A single crumb. A narrow gate. A tattered letter written months before.

"I'll write you back, just like I promised," Austin said. He tried to sound cheerful. "And maybe—"

But there was no maybe. That was all they had. It made Austin's chest ache until he thought he couldn't stand it.

Dinner that day was a quiet affair. No one seemed interested in the roasted chicken with corn pudding. The first two bites lodged in Austin's chest with the pain and wouldn't move. He put down his fork.

Although Aunt Olivia tried to get a conversation going about how much attention Polly was getting from the young men at the parties, no one else seemed to feel like talking either. Not even Polly herself. Aunt Olivia lapsed into a pouty silence.

When dinner was over, Austin was following Charlotte out of the dining room, hoping to have some time with her and Henry-James before the sun started to set. Uncle Drayton called him back.

"Would you sit down for just a moment, Austin?" he said. "I'd like to talk to you before you leave."

Austin looked longingly after Charlotte, but she signaled that she would wait outside. Austin sank into a chair beside his uncle at the head of the table.

"I have something I'd like for you to keep," Uncle Drayton said. "If you can fit it into your satchel, that is."

"Yes, sir?" Austin said.

"This was taken last summer. I'm glad now that I invited you to sit in for it. You've become as much a member of the family as Charlotte or Polly—"

"Or Kady" fell silently between them. That made Austin not quite sure he wanted whatever it was Uncle Drayton was pulling from inside his waistcoat. Until he saw it.

"I had this made up for you because I thought it might travel better than a big one," Uncle Drayton said. He presented a small brass case, about two-by-three inches in size, which opened like a book. On one side was a pad of red velvet. On the other, inside an oval mat of molded brass, was a picture of the Ravenal family—Aunt Olivia, Uncle Drayton, Kady, Polly, and Charlotte—and Austin, Jefferson, and Mother, taken at Canaan Grove on July 4th.

It was something Austin couldn't turn down. He held his hand out for it and felt the cold smooth metal in his palm.

"Thank you, sir," he said. "It will fit in my satchel. I'll keep it with my picture of my father." He looked up quickly. "I know you don't always agree with my father, but—"

Uncle Drayton put his hand on Austin's shoulder to stop him. "Your father is a good man, Austin," he said. "I may be angry with him sometimes. I may not understand everything he does or believes. But never let it be said that Wesley Hutchinson is not the best kind of man." He gave Austin's shoulder a squeeze. "And his son Austin is just like him."

"Drayton!" Aunt Olivia called from the hallway. "Come quickly! It's dreadful!"

Uncle Drayton sighed and excused himself from the table. Austin followed him, heart pounding again.

In the hallway, they found Aunt Olivia near to tears, fanning a bloated, red face with a small envelope.

"What is it?" Uncle Drayton said. "More bad news?"

"The worst!"

She thrust the envelope at her husband and stuck her face out at Mousie, who continued to fan her with her apron. Uncle Drayton's eyebrows puckered over the note he was reading.

"Is it about my father?" Austin said to him.

"Good heavens, no!" Aunt Olivia cried. "In fact, it's none of your business at all!"

"Nor is it mine," Uncle Drayton said. "Olivia, what is so upsetting about being invited to Mary Chesnut's for tea?"

Austin wasn't sure whether to laugh or scream. He didn't know how Uncle Drayton was keeping his temper.

"It is upsetting because I had planned to wear the wine-colored velvet hat I'm having made in Atlanta, the one with the ostrich plumes. It's identical to the riding hat designed for Empress Eugenie of France—and it hasn't arrived yet!"

"Olivia," Uncle Drayton said evenly, though Austin could hear him pulling back on his reins, "have we not more important things to worry about than your hat?"

"I must have *some* pleasure in the midst of all this

commotion!" Aunt Olivia cried. "I ask for so little."

"All right, all right!" he said. The voice was beginning to trumpet. "Henry-James!"

Henry-James stepped out of the shadows of the stairs and said, "Yes, Massa."

"Go to the train station and wait for today's shipment from Atlanta. If your missus's hat is there, bring it home directly." He looked at Aunt Olivia. "If it comes in today, you shall have it for tea, all right?"

"Bless you, Drayton," she said. She stepped forward to clasp his hands. Austin bolted up the stairs and met Charlotte at the landing.

"I know she's your mother," Austin hissed to her, "but she's a silly, silly woman! Now Henry-James is going to be gone all day. I wanted us to have just one more afternoon—"

Charlotte flapped her hands helplessly. She couldn't fix it. No one could fix it.

So the two of them spent most of the day on the joggling board, making up rhymes, quizzing each other with riddles, anything to keep from talking about what they wished would never happen.

The South Carolina sun splashed all over the garden, and Josephine brought them gingersnaps, and they both tried to laugh as much as they could. But everything was already beginning to look as if it didn't belong to him anymore, and Austin's chest ached. Charlotte's must have, too, because when the shadows started to get long, she suddenly burst out, "Don't go, Austin!"

Austin looked at her. She was miserably twisting her apron around her finger. She only did that when she was very upset.

"I don't want to go either," he said. "It isn't time."

"Can't you think of something? You always think of something."

"I tried. I can't."

"But why?"

She was talking like Jefferson used to when he didn't get his way. Austin thought for sure any minute she would stomp her foot. She recognized it, too, and she looked ashamed.

"I'm sorry. I just don't want you to go. I don't like it when we have to do what we don't want to do."

"I guess it's a narrow gate," he said.

"Narrow gate? You mean, like Daddy Elias used to talk about?" Austin nodded.

"I hate narrow gates," she said.

"I think I do, too."

"Who said you had to go through this one? Did Daddy Elias?"

"No, he just said doing what was right was sometimes like going through a narrow gate." He wriggled his shoulders. "The hard part is when you know something isn't right and you have to do it anyway. It's the same for Henry-James. Daddy Elias told him one thing, but that isn't what's right for Henry-James." And then he had a thought that surprised him. "I bet only Jesus can really tell you what to do! If He tells you, then it has to be right!"

Charlotte cocked her head at him. "But Daddy Elias knew all about Jesus. The only things I know about Jesus are what he told me."

"But he isn't here anymore," Austin said. His thoughts were pinging like hailstones in his head. "Maybe we have to know Jesus on our own now. And maybe He's gonna tell us something different from what he told Daddy Elias. Maybe we're different from him."

Charlotte frowned. "What do you mean?"

"Look at Kady," he said excitedly. "She's doing things differently from Aunt Olivia, and we think Kady's right, don't we?"

"Yes."

"And my mother did things differently from Uncle Drayton—"

"And we know how wise she is."

Austin sat up so straight on the joggling board that it bounced three times. "I know what to tell Henry-James!" he said. He grabbed Charlotte's wrist. "We have to go tell him! I want him to know before I leave."

"Tell him *what*, Austin?" she said. "Why is this so important?"

Austin opened his mouth—and then he closed it again. He couldn't tell Charlotte. She would never forgive him.

"Why don't you wait here?" he said. "I can run faster by myself."

"Run where?"

"To the train station—"

"It's all the way at the other end of town! You'll never make it and get back in time."

"Make it where?"

They looked up to see Kady standing at the garden gate.

Charlotte ran to her, the train station suddenly forgotten. Austin's chest seized up like it was in a vice. Kady was here. It was time to leave. There was no time left to do what he had to do.

"Are you ready, Austin?" she said over Charlotte's head.

Charlotte's eyes started to fill. Austin knew if he saw her face again, he'd be bawling, too. And he couldn't.

She still had her face buried in Kady's skirt when he went up behind her and said, "Good-bye, Charlotte. I'll wait for your first message."

She didn't answer him. He dragged himself into the house and got his satchel.

Until Jefferson and Austin hugged their mother upstairs and followed Kady down to the drawing room, Austin kept looking out the window for Henry-James to come back.

"Sometimes Jesus works just in the nick of time," his mother had said.

But Uncle Drayton was in the drawing room, ready to see them off. Acting as if Kady weren't even there, he shook hands with the boys and closed the door to the side piazza silently behind them. As they crossed the porch and climbed over the railing, Austin could still hear Aunt Olivia inside, whining because "that boy" hadn't returned from the train station with her hat. She'd missed her tea with Mary Chesnut.

"Oh, Mama," Kady whispered. "You'll never learn, will you?"

All the way to White Point Garden, Austin kept looking back over his shoulder, hoping Henry-James would return and run after them.

I can't leave without telling him what I found out—about the narrow gate, he thought. *I can't go!*

But they climbed into the wagon without him, Austin and Jefferson once more under the blanket in the back. Only the clip-clopping of the horse's hooves echoed over the quiet streets until they reached the wharf. Austin could hear Fitz talking softly to Kady, and soon the blanket was removed and Fitz lifted Jefferson out. There was no swashbuckling tonight, no flashing green eyes or wiggling eyebrows. He was very serious.

"The jolly boat is waitin' for us right down here," he whispered to them. "We'll row out to Sumter and be there by dawn—just in time to join the others. Are you bundled up?"

Austin nodded, and then he checked Jefferson's hat and scarf. His last promise to his mother had been to look after his little brother. Jefferson, for once, didn't seem to need much looking after. His face was pale, his eyes wide. He was too frightened to even make a peep.

"Don't be afraid, Jefferson," Kady whispered to him as they hurried down to the dock. "Fitz is a fine boatsman."

"I was never away from my mother before," Jefferson whispered back.

"Me neither," Kady said. "I know just how you feel."

The water looked like ink as they climbed into the little vessel and took their places on either side of Kady. Fitz sat behind them and took up the oars.

"Try and get some sleep now, lads," he said. "You've a long night ahead of you."

Jefferson at once wriggled down and put his head in Kady's lap. But Austin couldn't close an eye. He stared out over the water, which was lit by a lonely looking half moon, and watched Fort Sumter slowly draw nearer.

It was little more than a black mass across the water. Yet it was so important right now. It was the focus of everyone's attention, the center of something that was sure to lead to war.

And it's the last thing I'm going to see in South Carolina, Austin thought.

He looked away. That wasn't what he wanted to remember about his time here. He wanted to think about Canaan Grove and the swamp and Bogie—he hadn't gotten to say good-bye to Bogie—and Charlotte and Henry-James. He hadn't gotten to tell Henry-James what he now knew.

"Austin," Kady said to him, "do you know that I still have that letter you wrote to your friends the last time you were supposed to leave? Shall I still give it to them?"

Austin shook his head, and then he had an idea. "You can tell Henry-James something for me, though," he said. "And if he decides, you can promise to help him—"

But Kady put her hand on his arm and pointed across the harbor. "Fitz, what's that?" she said.

Fitz picked up a glass he had at his feet and focused it out into the harbor.

"It's a small steamship!" Fitz said. "It's sailing off from Fort Sumter, out to sea!"

"Already?" Kady said. "It wasn't supposed to leave until morning!"

Fitz didn't answer for a moment. He was squinting intently through the glass. When he put it down, Austin could see that his face was somber.

"It looks as if they've changed their minds," he said. "They've left in the dark of night, just like we did. They don't trust the Confederates, I suppose—and who can blame them, eh?"

Austin stared from Fitz to the steamship and back again.

"Does that mean they've left without us?" Austin said.

"That's what it means, lad," Fitz said. He pulled his oars out of the water and leaned on them. "Where to now?"

"You're asking me?" Austin said.

"I think it's up to you, Austin," Kady said. "We could take you on to the fort, though I don't know what they would do for you there now. This was the last chance for them to get their women and children to safety."

Austin sat staring into the water. *"Marse Jesus always gets the truth to you in time,"* Daddy Elias had told him. *And Mother agreed. She told me I was good enough and didn't even know it. She said all I had to do was believe—*

Then where is it? Austin thought. *Where are the words to tell me what to do?*

There were no words.

But there was a feeling. A feeling of being a good person, and knowing that God was pushing the right gate open. He wasn't sure how he knew. He just did.

"Take us back to the townhouse," Austin said. "If Jefferson and I have to hide, then we'll hide. I know my father will find a way to get us back to the North."

"That's what it shall be then," Fitz said.

He dipped the oars back into the water and paddled the boat around. Kady let her eyes fall softly on Austin.

"You look awfully happy, Austin," she said. "This is only for a little while, you know."

"It's long enough," Austin said. "A little while is all I need."

There was a huge commotion back at the townhouse when they arrived. Aunt Olivia looked even angrier than she had about her silly hat, and Charlotte couldn't seem to decide whether to laugh or cry, so she did both at once. His mother knew exactly what she wanted to do. Austin had never seen her sob so hard, as if she'd been holding back the whole Ashley River behind her eyes.

But the person Austin really wanted to see was Henry-James. He found him out in the stable, listlessly grooming one of Uncle Drayton's horses. When he saw Austin, he dropped the currycomb and rushed to him almost as if he were going to throw his arms right around Austin's neck. They both took a hurried step back and then stood there looking at each other.

"You back to stay, Massa Austin?" Henry-James said.

Austin shook his head. "No, but never mind that. I have something really important to tell you."

"Jus' about everything you say is important, Massa Austin," Henry-James said. He grinned more readily than usual. "Leastwise, you thinks so."

"No, this is *really* important. I think this comes from God, and it's about you, Henry-James."

Henry-James's face grew sober. He nodded slowly and leaned against the stable wall with his arms crossed. "Go on then, Massa Austin," he said.

"You remember when Daddy Elias used to talk about the narrow gate and how you thought you had to go through the same one he did because he knew all about Jesus?"

"That's truth," Henry-James said. His eyes started to go stony.

"I don't think that's what he really meant!" Austin said. "I thought of this—well, actually, God told me—oh, I don't know! But this is how I think it is, Henry-James. We have to go through the gate Jesus tells us to—you and me and Kady, all separate— because people all have their *own* narrow gate! No matter how hard it is and no matter who says we shouldn't, we have to do it. I think God made it so I could come back and tell you that."

Henry-James grew so still that Austin wasn't sure he was even breathing. Finally, he said, "You think the Lord really want me to do what I feel like my insides is tellin' me to do?"

"I do," Austin said.

There was another statue-still pause. Then Henry-James shook his head. "Miz Lottie ain't gonna like this."

"I know," Austin said. "That's why I didn't even tell her. The gate you have to pick isn't the one she'd choose for you, that's for sure. Polly's the same way about Tot." Austin leaned in hard toward Henry-James. "But it's your gate, Henry-James. And if Jesus is telling you to go through it, you have to find a way."

"Miz Kady, she could help me," Henry-James said.

"She's perfect! And I could help some, too."

Even in the dark, Austin could see Henry-James's eyes droop. "But you ain't gonna be here much longer, Massa Austin. Some way or 'nother, you gots to get out of South Carolina."

"I know," Austin said, "but I've got long enough, I just know it."

Henry-James smiled until Austin could see the gap between his teeth. He seemed to know what Austin knew now—that it didn't take long to get through a narrow gate once you knew it was yours.

✝ ✟ ✝

There's More Adventure in the CHRISTIAN HERITAGE SERIES!

The Salem Years, 1689–1691

The Rescue #1

Josiah and his older sister, Hope, used to fight a lot. But now, she's very sick. And neither the town doctor nor all the family's wishing can save her. Their only earthly chance is an old widow—a stranger to Salem Village—whose very presence could destroy the family's relationship with everyone else! Can she save Hope? And at what price?

The Stowaway #2

Josiah is going to town! Sent to Salem Town to be educated, Josiah Hutchinson's dream of someday becoming a sailor now seems within reach. But a tough orphan named Simon has other plans, and his evil schemes could get both Josiah and Hope in a heap of trouble. How will the kids prove their innocence? Whose story will the village believe?

The Guardian #3

Josiah has heard the wolves howling at night, and he's devised a way of dealing with them. But with the perfect night to execute the plan approaching, there's still one not-so-small problem—Cousin Rebecca, who follows Josiah around like his shadow . . . even into danger! How will Josiah protect her? What will happen to the wolves?

The Accused #4

Josiah Hutchinson is robbed by the cruel Putnam brothers! In a desperate attempt to retrieve his stolen property, he's accused of being the thief and unexpectedly finds himself on trial for crimes he didn't commit! Can Josiah find the courage to tell the truth? Will anyone believe him if he does? Will he be torn from his family and locked away in a dingy jail cell?

The Samaritan #5

Taking to heart a message he heard at church, Josiah attempts to help a starving old widow and her daughter. But while he's trying hard to forge new friendships, the feud with the Putnams is getting out of control. Will Josiah be clever enough to escape their wicked ways? Can God protect him when it seems hopeless?

The Secret #6

Hope's got a crush on someone—and Josiah knows who it is! Can he keep it a secret? After all, if Papa found out who she's been sneaking away to see, he'd be furious! And if the Putnams find out, who knows what will happen!

The Williamsburg Years, 1780–1781

The Rebel #1

The Hutchinson family history continues in the first book of the Williamsburg Years. Josiah's great-grandson, Thomas, doesn't think he'll ever like Williamsburg. Things get worse when the apothecary shop he works in is robbed! Thomas thinks he knows who did it, but before he can prove it, he's accused of the crime and taken to jail. How will he convince everyone he's innocent?

The Thief #2

Horses are being stolen in Williamsburg! And after Thomas sees a masked rider leading a horse, he believes it's Nicholas, the new doctor who has come to town. When Thomas's friend is seriously injured, Thomas knows the young doctor may be his friend's only chance. Can he trust Nicholas to take care of him?

The Burden #3

Thomas Hutchinson knows secrets, but he can't tell anyone! And he soon learns that "bearing one another's burdens," as he heard in church, is not always easy—especially when a crazed Walter Clark holds him at gunpoint for a secret he doesn't even know! Will Walter ever believe Thomas? How will he be freed of these secrets?

The Prisoner #4

War in Williamsburg is raging! But when Thomas's mentor, Nicholas, refuses to fight, he is carried off against his will by the Patriots. Witnessing this harsh treatment, Thomas feels confused and trapped. Whose side should he be on? Will he ever understand what it means to be free?

The Invasion #5

When word arrives that Benedict Arnold and his men are ransacking plantations nearby, Thomas, his family and friends return to their homestead to protect it. But British soldiers break in, taking food, horses, and Caroline as hostage! Now what? Will Thomas be able to help straighten out this horrible situation?

The Battle #6

Though the war is all around him, Thomas is more frustrated by the *internal* fighting he feels. He's expected to take orders from a woman he doesn't like, he's forbidden to talk about his missing brother, Sam, and, to top it all off, he's not getting along with two of his closest friends. Will nothing turn out right?

The Charleston Years, 1860–1861

The Misfit #1

When the crusade to abolish slavery reaches full swing, Austin

Hutchinson (Thomas's great-grandson) is sent to live with relatives. But he's not sure he'll enjoy his stay because his cousins—Kady, Polly, and Charlotte—don't seem to like him. Even Henry-James, the slave boy, wants nothing to do with him. Will Austin ever find his place?

The Ally #2

When Austin discovers that Henry-James can't read, Austin resolves to teach him—even though it's illegal to educate slaves. But that only leads to trouble! Uncle Drayton is furious when he realizes Henry-James has secretly been given lessons and locks him in an old shack until he can be sold. Can Austin free Henry-James without getting them into more trouble? Will he able to forgive Uncle Drayton for being so harsh?

The Threat #3

Trouble has a way of following Austin wherever he goes! First, while traveling to the Ravenals' vacation home, he overhears two men scheming against his Uncle Drayton and spies a lanky boy tampering with the family's stagecoach. Then, while playing one afternoon near the church, Austin and Charlotte have a run-in with the same boy and his brother! Can Austin find peace amidst all the hostility?

The Trap #4

During the annual harvest festival at the Ravenal plantation, Austin's slave friend Henry-James beats a hired hand named Narvel in a wrestling match. Narvel is furious—and determined to get even! He picks a fight with Henry-James, gets Charlotte in trouble . . . and even traps Austin in a water well. Can Narvel's mischief be stopped? Can Austin convince Uncle Drayton that it's Narvel—and not Henry-James—who's causing all the trouble?

Available at a Christian bookstore near you

FOCUS ON THE FAMILY®

Like this book?

Then you'll love *Clubhouse* magazine! It's written for kids just like you, and it's loaded with great stories, interesting articles, puzzles, games, and fun things for you to do. Some issues include posters, too! With your parents' permission, we'll even send you a complimentary copy.

Simply write to Focus on the Family, Colorado Springs, CO 80995 (in Canada, write P.O. 9800, Stn. Terminal, Vancouver, B.C. V6B 4G3) and mention that you saw this offer in the back of this book. Or, call 1-800-A-FAMILY (in Canada, call 1-800-661-9800).

You may also visit our Web site (www.family.org) to learn more about the ministry or find out if there is a Focus on the Family office in your country.

•   •   •

"Adventures in Odyssey" is a fantastic series of books, videos, and radio dramas that's fun for the entire family—parents, too! You'll love the twists and turns found in the novels, as well as the excitement packed into every video. And the 30 albums of radio dramas (available on audiocassette or compact disc) are great to listen to in the car, after dinner . . . even at bedtime! You can hear "Adventures in Odyssey" on the radio, too. Call Focus on the Family for a listing of local stations airing these programs or to request any of the "Adventures in Odyssey" resources. They're also available at Christian bookstores everywhere.

Focus on the Family is an organization that is dedicated to helping you and your family establish lasting, loving relationships with each other and the Lord. It's why we exist! If we can assist you or your family in any way, please feel free to contact us. We'd love to hear from you!